ENCHANTMENTS AND THE EERILY ENSNARED

A WILLIAMS WITCH MYSTERY

BOOK SEVEN

ELOISE EVERHART

ALORIUM PUBLISHING

This is a work of fiction. Names, characters, places, and incidents either are the product of the author's imagination or are used fictitiously, and any resemblance to actual persons, living or dead, business establishments, events, or locales is entirely coincidental.

PB ISBN: 978-1-962759-06-9

Author: Eloise Everhart

Editors: Rashida Breen and Kelly Reed

Cover design by GetCovers

CHAPTER 1

Wind buffeted the car, causing it to sway around me. I gritted my teeth as I forced myself to keep my eyes unfocused on the darkened street. Fighting back nausea, I concentrated on the green line in front of me. The tendril of magical energy had started at my house and crept its way into town, its path meandering back and forth like a stream. It had been caused by a spell cast by a malicious entity, a Fae creature known as the Outsider, that had taken over my daughter's body. When I told the Retirees about the tendrils, they'd bickered back and forth over what it could mean. Sarah had suggested that it was a poisoning of something she called a ley line, which traveled under my house. She argued that we should focus on the corruption at the house instead of focusing on the lines. The tingling at the back of my neck told me she was wrong. Fortunately, Betty and Agnes had overruled her, and we had decided, as a group, to investigate where the lines went. However, they may have voted in my favor because they could tell I would refuse to believe the lines meant nothing. The shimmering green light emanating from my house and seeping into town was the only lead I had to rescue my daughter.

"Turn left," I said.

Chris grunted in acknowledgement and turned at the next intersection.

Keeping my eyes unfocused made driving unsafe, and stopping and starting had proven to be time-consuming. Fortunately, Chris had volunteered to help. He couldn't see the lines. They were something only a witch could find and only if she knew what to look for. But after I'd come clean to him about my witchly heritage, he hadn't questioned me on the strange things I had to do. Showing up with a bag at one in the morning, claiming something had possessed my daughter, and I needed someplace to stay? Reasonable. Driving me around town, following an invisible line? He would do it. Warmth spread through my chest. He had more faith in me than my ex-husband ever had. I still wasn't sure what I had done to deserve Chris.

The line in front of me swerved to the right, cutting straight through a house. I patted his leg and pointed. He took the next available turn. He slowed as my head swiveled back and forth as I tried to find the line again. It had exited the house at an odd angle and cut down an alleyway.

"There." I pointed.

He slammed on his brakes to make a tight right turn, and my seat belt tightened around me. We slid into the alleyway, and he slowed his pace even further. We crawled forward at about ten miles an hour.

Motion caught my eye. I blinked and looked up in time to see a squirrel leap from one roof to another. The house cat that had been chasing it skidded to a halt and hissed. The squirrel scampered away into the darkness. I exhaled and shook myself. My seat belt wouldn't let me move forward. I quickly unclipped it and let it slide back into place before rebuckling it.

Chris came to a stop at the end of the alley. The tendril didn't continue to the other side of the street.

Chris looked both ways down the T-intersection. "Where now?"

I rolled my shoulders back and unfocused my eyes again. *Let me see.* The green line shimmered into view on my second long exhalation. It twisted to the left. I pointed.

Chris inched forward into the intersection and turned. We drove past the last of the suburbs. We were headed into the heart of downtown. Single-family homes were replaced by rows of brownstones and businesses. As we approached the pier, the green vein darted off to the right again.

"Turn here," I said.

We followed the line, twisting and turning through the streets of downtown Point Pleasant. It was well past dusk, and the last of the dinnertime stragglers had returned to their cars hours before. I leaned forward in my seat and stared at the green sparkles as they dipped inside another building. It was the old sheriff's station that had been abandoned years before, after a water leak forced them to evacuate.

"Circle the block. I don't see which way it comes out," I said.

Chris turned right. We coasted down and around the block, his foot barely on the gas. I followed the building with my neck as I kept my eyes unfocused. The green line plunged into the building through the front doors, and it didn't come back out.

"Which way?" Chris asked as we pulled back up to the front.

"I didn't see it come out." I fidgeted in my seat. "Could you go around again? Just in case?"

The car slid forward. He drove even more slowly that time around. We were going so slowly that a pedestrian could have passed us. Even at that pace, I didn't see the green tendril come back out. It had gone inside the old sheriff's station and stopped.

"It ends in there." I cocked my head toward the station.

Chris pulled into the parking lot. The concrete was cracked, and weeds poked out of the fissures. We came to a stop facing the doors. Even from there, I could see the white notice from the city, taped to the door to declare it temporarily condemned. The ink was faded. When the notice was posted five years before, they hadn't planned on the relocation to the double-wides just outside town being a permanent solution. But as with all construction projects in the region, starting always took longer than anticipated—or getting the budget approved when the temporary solution worked well enough.

I leaned forward in my seat and craned my neck back. The three-story building loomed over me, its windows dark. The ones on the ground floor had been boarded up, the plywood slipped in between the glass and the metal bars. I grimaced. *Why does the light have to end here?*

"Now what?" Chris reached across the center console and squeezed my hand.

"I need to go in." I unclipped my seat belt.

He held on to me. "Are you sure that's a good idea?"

I glanced between him and the building. The green tendril of magical energy went there for a reason. I had to know why. "No… but do I have a choice?"

"Putting aside that it's breaking and entering," Chris said as he held my gaze, "you don't have any protective gear on you. It was condemned for a reason. Mold."

I slumped in my seat.

"But—"

My head snapped up toward him.

He held up a finger. "The renovation project is scheduled to start tomorrow."

I blinked. I had almost forgotten about the project. Only a few days had passed since I promised Olivia I would help out with that. Her father, the mayor of Point Pleasant, wanted someone he trusted to represent the city with the various contractors, not only to make sure the project stayed reasonably close to the budget and on track but to make sure it was done right the first time. While I wasn't a contractor, all my years as a property claims adjuster had taught me a thing or two about keeping restoration projects moving. Step one was the mold remediation work. Tomorrow, they would begin gutting the building.

"And I can go inside then," I whispered. A smile spread across my face.

He nodded.

My phone dinged in my pocket. I fished it out.

> **HEATHER:**
> Everyone else is back. Are you done tracking down your lines?

> **DANI:**
> Just finished. Heading over now.

I snapped a picture of the old sheriff's station and slid my phone back into place. Chris backed out of the parking lot. I stared at the building as we drove away. It lay at the end of one of the eight tendrils that emanated from my home. The Retirees had taken three, Megan Miller had taken another two, and I had taken the last three. And Heather was quarterbacking the operation from her apartment over the Bizzy Bean. This was the last tendril. My heart clenched as we pulled up in front of the cafe.

"Thank you for driving me around today," I said.

Chris squeezed my hand. "Anytime. I hope one of you found what you were looking for."

"Me too." I kissed him. "Don't wait up. I might be a while. See you when I get home."

I flushed when he smiled at the word *home.* It had slipped out. I had spent only one night at his house, but I already felt more comfortable there than I did at my place. To be fair, my home was under a magical spell that made anyone inside feel impatient and moody. Feeling comfortable somewhere else wasn't difficult. But to call Chris's place home felt right. *Have we really taken that much of a next step?*

"I'll keep the light on for you," he murmured.

I ducked my head and slipped out of the car. He chuckled as I closed the car door. I hunched my shoulders and shoved my hands into my pockets. I fingered his house key in my pocket as I trudged up to the Bizzy Bean.

Chris backed out of the parking space as I pulled the front door open. Warmth flooded over me, chasing away the midnight chill. The other women had already arrived and were crowded around one of the round tables in the plexiglass cat enclosure to the left. I pulled the door closed behind me and made my way to their table.

A large map of the town, fastened to a corkboard, sat in the middle of the table. The Retirees sat on one side of the table, and Megan stood a few feet away, reading from a piece of paper as Heather pushed a pin into place on the map.

"And the other one ended at 1482 Eddison Avenue. It's three blocks north, two blocks east from the other one." Megan dropped her notepad into her purse.

"Another home?" Betty asked.

"All occupied too." Megan flopped into a chair. "I got some weird looks when one of the neighbors saw me staring at the place, but that's no surprise. One of you ladies might have better luck getting an invitation inside."

Other than Heather, all the women at the table were witches. And we had all descended from the same cursed coven. Megan's curse was probably the worst of the bunch. Betty couldn't cast magic without something going wrong. Agnes couldn't leave Point Pleasant without getting deathly ill. Sarah could cast spells only on the full moon. I had prophetic dreams of the future, which I had no control over. But Megan was instantly distrusted by anyone she met or even heard her name. Hers was a lonely life. Until recently, she hadn't had any friends.

"My first two were homes as well but not the last one." I stepped up next to Heather and grabbed the push pins from her. I shoved them quickly into place. "The last place I checked, the line ended at the old sheriff's station."

"That has to mean something, right?" Betty asked.

Sarah shrugged. "Not necessarily. It's not uncommon for ley lines to go through buildings with history."

I grabbed a seat from a nearby table and sat down with the group. We stared down at the map. Several of the points were clustered in the same neighborhood. But the others were spread out over the town. I could see no rhyme or reason to any of it.

"The only way to know is to go inside," Agnes said.

Betty shuddered. "Abandoned buildings always creeped me out."

"It's not going to be abandoned for long," Sarah said.

I nodded. "I think I have an in for that."

The group turned and looked at me.

"It's part of Steven Bishop's revitalization project."

He was the new town mayor. He'd hit the ground running with his plans to rebuild the downtown.

"I volunteered to help him with it. Demo work starts tomorrow."

"What's the plan once you get inside?" Betty asked.

I shrugged, for I was in uncharted territory. Being a witch still felt new to me. Only seven months had passed since I found out. And every month, I learned something new that turned my world upside down again. Planning was hard when I didn't know what would change on me next.

The Retirees exchanged a glance. This was new territory for them as well. They'd been cursed for so long that they'd accepted it. Taking it into account was no different to them than grocery shopping or scheduling a hair appointment.

Our discovery of the origins of the curse—and my daughter's subsequent possession by one of the entities responsible—had turned their lives inside out as well. We were all floundering.

The clock over the door ticked away the seconds as we sat in silence, staring at the map. The sound was a constant reminder of how little time we had left. A Warden of the West, one of the secret police of the witching world, would arrive in two days. We'd spent a whole day tracking down the lines. We had a little over a day to figure things out.

Heather cleared her throat. "What are we going to do about Grace?"

The question was like a bomb going off. I flinched. The Retirees grimaced, and Megan pulled away from us, her arms wrapping around her stomach. She had been the one to call the Wardens. She had to. She was under a mind-compulsion spell to report information to them. That probably didn't make her feel any less guilty.

"Ask me again tomorrow," I said.

CHAPTER 2

I lay in bed next to Chris, staring up at the ceiling. He'd been asleep when I got back to his place. He had woken up long enough to pull me into a hug when I climbed into bed. He was presently snoring gently next to me, his head resting against mine, his arm thrown across my stomach. I'd barely slept all night but not because I wasn't comfortable. His bed was plush, and I was nice and warm under the covers. The reason was the unknown. The question Heather had asked replayed through my mind. *What are we going to do about Grace?* I hated feeling lost. I rechecked my front door Ring camera on my phone. Her car was still parked in her usual spot. I squeezed my eyes shut. I would give almost anything to know what the right answer to that question was.

My phone jingled in my hands. I turned off the alarm.

"Five more minutes," Chris grumbled. He wrapped his arm more tightly around me as I tried to inch toward the edge of the bed.

"I've gotta get up." I turned and sank into his arms.

"In five more minutes," he said.

I blocked out the uncertainty of the day and closed my eyes. For five minutes, I embraced the feeling of being content. But as my alarm chimed again, I sighed and extricated myself from the covers.

I padded down two short flights of stairs to the narrow living room. Chris's townhome was cozy. While everything was narrower than I was used to, he had strategically placed furniture to make the space feel bigger than it was. I hadn't unpacked my night bag yet. It sat on the couch with half its contents poking out at odd angles. I fished out a change of clothes and went through the motions: shower, clothes, followed by breakfast for myself and my cat familiar, Charlie. I scratched his head as I mentally went through the plan for the day. Everything started and stopped with getting inside the old sheriff's station. I had been so distracted lately that I didn't know which mold remediation company was taking the lead. I had to talk to Olivia first. Charlie could sense my unease and headbutted my hand. He purred as he walked back and forth in front of me. Through our bond, I could feel his uncertainty, though. He didn't know if it was going to be all right either.

At twenty minutes to seven, I packed up my purse, said goodbye to Charlie for the day, and headed out the door. He objected to my leaving him behind but relented when I told him a construction site was no place for a cat. I could still sense his moodiness as I drove through town.

Going into work from another direction felt odd. If not for my house being under the effects of a strange spell, I wasn't sure I would've had the nerve to sleep over at Chris's so soon. That was a blessing in disguise, in a way. I couldn't drive to the office on autopilot. I had to think about each turn, which kept the anxious energy in my mind at bay.

Olivia was walking up to our shared office building as I pulled up. With the changing weather, Olivia had put her hair into cornrows, the long braids piled on the top of her head in a bun. Her bright-red coat flared around her legs as she walked. In one hand she grasped a rolling cart piled high with boxes, and in the other she held the leash for Bailey, her golden-haired dog with a wide, smiling face.

I clambered out of the car and scurried after her. "Hey, Liv, you need a hand with that?"

Olivia beamed at me as I caught up to her as Bailey bounced around us, her tail going a mile a minute. "That would be great. I was dreading juggling the door, the cart, and Bailey."

I grabbed the handle of the cart from Olivia and followed her the rest of the way. I had inherited the brick building from my grandmother. Olivia rented an office space on one side for her Pleasant View Insurance Agency, and I worked across our shared foyer in my office for Williams Adjusting. I trailed after her as she made her way into her half of the building.

"I heard the demo work at the sheriff's station is starting today," I said.

Olivia nodded. "You've been so busy lately I haven't had a chance to talk to you about it again. Are you still okay with helping out my dad with the reconstruction project?"

"Yeah. I wouldn't dream of backing out now." I helped Olivia unpack the cart. "I was actually thinking it would be a good idea if I was involved from the beginning. Do you think it would be all right if I popped over during the demolition work?"

"Of course!" Olivia bounced in place, a smile spreading across her face. She reached out and grabbed my arm. "I'm so glad you're involved. My dad has been stressing out about this all week. He's convinced he's going to fall flat on his face with his first big project as mayor. And you've seemed a little distracted with work and Chris. I assume all the time you've been spending together means things are going well?"

I flushed. If she knew where I'd spent the night, she would want to know all the details. She would probably be disappointed by the facts: we just slept peacefully in each other's arms.

"I just take my job seriously," I said.

Olivia raised her eyebrow. "Something happened, didn't it?"

"Nothing," I sputtered. "Yet."

Her grin widened, and she playfully swatted at my shoulder. "Dost thou protest too much?"

I chuckled and shook my head. "We are back together. But that doesn't change the fact that I take my job seriously. Who would I need to call to get access? I missed the project briefing."

Olivia pulled out her phone. "I'll call my dad."

I stepped aside as Olivia talked to her father. Bailey followed me, close at my heels. She'd been waiting patiently next to us the entire time, her eager face staring up at us. My heart wasn't in it as I crouched next to her. As if she could sense my mood, she doubled her efforts at being adorable. She exploded with energy as she leaped up and pushed her cold nose against my cheek. I pushed her back gently, and she dropped her head into a playful bow. She bounced from foot to foot. To keep up appearances in front of Olivia, I grabbed one of Bailey's toys from under a nearby desk and tossed it. Bailey snatched it out of the air and skittered forward so I could grab the other end. We were in the midst of an intense tug-of-war when Olivia cleared her throat.

I glanced up at her. "What does he have to say?"

"He said you should just stop by around lunchtime. The project manager just got on-site and is doing a walk-through. They are marking things to demolish and should start on that this afternoon."

"That's perfect. It'll be good for me to see it before and after." I stood and brushed off my pants.

"Thanks again for being so involved." Olivia pulled me into a hug. "It means a lot to me. And my dad."

I returned the hug. "Anytime."

She stepped back and sat down at her desk.

"I should probably get to work. Those reports aren't going to write themselves." I cocked my head toward the cart filled with boxes. "And it looks like you've got your hands full yourself."

"It's renewal season. I swear there's something about the new year that makes people rethink their policies. It's always nuts in the first quarter."

I scratched Bailey behind her ears then walked across the foyer to my office. I did have reports to write, but I wasn't sure how well I would be able to focus on them with everything going on with Grace. I rechecked the Ring camera on my phone. Her car hadn't moved. She was still at home. *Please let there be answers at the station. I need you to be okay.*

I wasn't sure how I'd done it, but I'd managed to force myself to focus until lunch. I powered through report after report and got them out to the insurance companies ahead of schedule. But with each file I finished, at least two new assignments came in. I politely declined the ones I could afford to turn down. As much as I wanted to focus solely on my daughter, I was self-employed. If I didn't work, I didn't eat. I accepted a few jobs that could wait until the next week then closed my laptop. My desk was clear of anything time sensitive, so I could afford to take a few days off. I grabbed my bag and headed out.

Although I didn't need it, I turned on my GPS and followed it to the old sheriff's station. Listening to the voice telling me where to turn kept my mind from doom spiraling. Grace meant everything to me. The idea of losing her was paralyzing. I had to stay focused on the next step, or I would freeze out of fear.

I rolled to a stop outside the old sheriff's station. I found a space behind a white work truck parked out front and got out of my car. Sometime in the morning, an oversize dumpster had been delivered. It took up almost a quarter of the parking lot. The boards had been taken off the building's windows, revealing dirty glass. I craned my neck as my eyes traveled up to the roof. In the daylight, the building looked forlorn. The rain had worn away at the brick facade in places, making it look like the windows had tracks of tears trailing down the siding. Moss clung to the windowsills and gutters. The place desperately needed a good power washing.

The front door was open, and muffled voices floated to me on the breeze. I stamped my feet to keep them warm as I donned the protective gear I'd stashed in my trunk. The last thing to go on was the protective gloves. I fiddled with them until they covered the cuffs of my shirt. As I walked up to the building, I pushed my respirator into place.

The foyer wasn't too bad. Weak sunlight streamed through the windows. The air was stale, and a layer of dust covered every surface. Thick plastic sheets were taped across the entrance to the hall, sealing away whatever contaminants lay beyond.

I unfocused my eyes and willed myself to see the unseen. The green tendril of magic I'd followed the night before cut through the room and went straight through the hanging plastic. I slipped through it in the appropriate place and froze. The next room was awful.

Half the ceiling was gone. In the few places the drywall had not completely failed, it hung in clumps. The exposed floorboards of the room above were blackened with mold. The walls of the room were stained. The entire room would need to be gutted. I swallowed, pushing down the bile gathering at the back of my throat. I'd seen a lot of mold in my day, but it never got any less gross looking. At least this stuff looked dry, the water long gone.

The green tendril of light flowed through the room and down a hallway to the left, toward the sound of voices. I followed it into the next room. As I followed the line, I couldn't shut my adjuster brain off. Even with my eyes unfocused, I could tell it wasn't as bad past the hall, but all the drywall would still need to come down due to the proximity. Little blue tape marks littered the walls, indicating cut lines.

I followed the green tendril as it wound its way through the building. I walked down corridors, through long-abandoned rooms, and past work crews diligently taping the walls to show where they intended to cut into the drywall. They seemed to be planning to flood cut most of the first floor by taking out the lowest two feet of drywall in every room. However, when I got to the back of the building, in the rooms farthest from the leak, the tape marks were more sporadic, and some entire rooms hadn't been marked.

The green line went straight into a wall. I peeked into the adjoining room and out the window in the back. The line didn't reappear. It entered the wall and vanished. I glanced around the room. A few tape marks were on the wall closest to the hallway, but nothing marked the wall where the light disappeared. I chewed on my lip and stuck my head out into the hallway. A work crew was two doors down, applying the last few bits of tape. That was the last room they had to check before the project manager did his walk-through.

Music played out of a plastic-wrapped speaker perching on a filing cabinet behind them. Next to it was a toolbox, where they'd stashed their moisture meter and extra rolls of tape. I glanced between the roll of tape and the wall where the green line disappeared. I had to know. *What if the answer to freeing Grace is behind that wall?*

I tiptoed down the hall and snagged a roll of tape from the pile then darted back into the room. I moved quickly, my head swiveling between my task and the open door behind me. The workers could finish up with their job at any second and walk past the room. I tore off strips of tape and stuck them to the walls of the room, indicating that room needed to be flood cut as well. If I put the marks higher, the project manager might question it. Two feet would have to do. I hoped I could see what I needed to with that much visibility. And if not, I would have to get creative.

I leaned out into the hallway. The workers were still finishing up their section. I sneaked up behind them and dropped the roll of tape back into the toolbox before they noticed it was missing, and I walked back out of the building to wait.

The project manager arrived twenty minutes later.

"Dani, it's so good to see you," Sam said.

Over the past few months, I'd handled a few water damage claims on which Sam was the lead. He was an amiable-enough guy and was strict with his workers. He didn't put up with nonsense on the job site. That made working with him as an adjuster a good experience. He always had what I needed.

"Sam! I didn't know you were on this one, or I would have messaged you directly." I shook his hand.

We chatted as I followed him through the job site. He was quick and methodical, going from room to room. He added a piece of tape here and there. As we entered the room the light had led me to, I held my breath as he checked the tape. He cocked his head to the side as he stared at the tape marks.

"There were water lines in the hall," I said.

He shrugged. "You're right. It will probably need to come out anyway. This place is riddled with mold."

I exhaled as he stepped out of the room and finished up his walk-through. The room had stayed on the demolition plan.

"Where were you planning on starting?" I followed him back to the front room.

"At the front, and then we'll move back." He checked off his inspection from his to-do list.

"How long do you think it'll take?"

"We have a cold front moving in on Sunday, and it's always all hands on deck after those. I want to get the first floor done today and then move up. Filter the air and then do some clearance mold testing. The goal is to get it wrapped up by Saturday if all goes well."

"Excellent. Mind if I stick around and watch?"

He shrugged. "It'll be boring, but suit yourself."

We stood in companionable silence as he finished up his paperwork. He was signing off on the last page as more work crews pulled up outside. He really had timed things perfectly.

They got to work quickly. I stood out of the way and watched as they tore drywall down, wrapped it in plastic, and hauled it outside to the dump. They worked in sequence. One team tore things down, the next disposed of the material, and the last sprayed antimicrobial agents on the newly cleared space. The first room took the longest, then they rapidly moved from room to room, clearing things out. It was fascinating to watch.

Even at their rapid pace, the time ticked away. Before I knew it, the sun had dipped below the horizon, and the rooms were dark. They pulled out LED work lights to brighten the space. The time was almost five when they came to a stop outside *the room*. I stared at them in dismay as they packed up their stuff.

"There're only two more rooms left. You sure you don't want to finish up the first floor today?" I asked Sam.

He shrugged. I couldn't let him stop right then.

I took a gamble and appealed to his pride. "Or are you really okay with falling behind schedule on the first day?"

He narrowed his eyes and turned toward his workers. "It's two more rooms. Get 'em done."

I hovered in the doorway as the workers cut through the

drywall. My palms became sweaty as they neared the spot in the wall the green line had disappeared into. I unfocused my eyes and stared at the point in the wall where the line vanished. I found myself holding my breath as they made the first cut into the wall. My hands shook as I exhaled.

Their bodies blocked where the line disappeared. I craned my neck, trying to see, as the workers made the last cut into the drywall. They pulled it down and screamed. They scrambled back on their elbows. I stared in horror. The green line ended at a skull.

CHAPTER 3

The group fled the room. Sam grabbed my arm and pulled me to the lobby, where he called 911. We stood, huddled in groups, in the lobby, waiting for the sheriff to show up. I hugged my arms to my body. Something was ironic about calling the sheriff to a crime scene at their own station.

I leaned against the wall. Sam paced a few feet away, muttering under his breath. He was more concerned with the schedule than with the body. Work would halt until the scene was cleared, and things moved slowly in Point Pleasant. Weeks might pass before they could finish the demolition.

The front door slammed open, and Bob, the local sheriff, strode inside. Chris and Harrison, the other deputy, trailed after him. Bringing up the rear was Victor, the local medical examiner. The sheriff and his deputies were all in uniform. Harrison, the tallest of the bunch, ducked his head so that he wouldn't hit it on the doorframe. He hunched in an attempt to make his long, gangly body seem less awkward. Victor was the only one suited up for being around mold. His usual regency suit had been replaced with something close to a hazmat suit, minus the giant headpiece. He had the hood up, pinned into place by a respirator, covering his graying pompadour and distinctive beard. He stopped briefly for directions then strode back through the plastic sheet to inspect the body.

Bob stiffened when he noticed me. He glowered and turned away. "Anyone who was not in the room when the body was discovered, please give your name and number to Deputy Harrison. Afterward, you may leave. If we have questions, we'll contact you."

I stayed put.

Bob glanced over his shoulder at me and sighed. "Of course you were in the room."

I grimaced. Someday, he would stop hating me. But today was not that day.

"Chris, start with Miss Williams. I'll start with the gentleman who called it in, and we'll go from there. Harrison, when you're done getting contact information, tape off the scene."

Chris walked over to me, flipping open a notepad. "A body, huh?"

"Yeah. I didn't see much." I couldn't keep the disappointment out of my voice. I'd come to get answers.

"Would it be helpful for you to walk me through it and show me where you were standing?" Chris had a twinkle in his eye.

I smiled at him. A second look at the scene would be helpful.

I nodded. "I have extra masks if you need one."

I ran out to my car to get him a respirator mask then led him through the building to where the body had been located. Victor was inspecting what he could see of the body through the opening. I pointed at where I'd been standing. "I was here when it happened."

I very slowly went through the events, explaining in great detail everything that had happened. Chris let me talk. He stood angled away from me so that I had a clear view into the room. I watched as Victor cut more of the drywall back to access the body. It had been wrapped in canvas, which was stained dark either from mold or from blood. He took a few photos before moving the body out and unwrapping it.

How on earth had a body been in there without someone noticing? Wouldn't it have stunk? I scrunched up my nose. The only thing I could think of was that that section didn't have central air, so the smell would've been contained to the area. That—combined with the fact that the room was a storage closet, which wouldn't have had a lot of foot traffic—could mean no one had noticed. My stomach roiled as I imagined how bad it could've smelled near the wall. *A lot of air fresheners, too, maybe?*

Bob came up behind me. He grunted, and I scrambled out of his way. He strode past me into the room without giving me a second glance. "What do we have? Got a cause of death yet?"

"Too early to tell." Victor crouched next to the skeleton. He touched the skull. "Based on the cracks, probably some sort of head trauma."

"Any idea how long it's been in there?"

Victor peeled back more of the canvas. The body was still clothed. It was wearing high-waisted pants with a button-up shirt, a waistcoat, and a jacket over the top. Victor carefully patted down the body. He paused over the hips then reached into a pocket and pulled out a leather wallet. He flipped it open and with steady fingers slipped a small rectangular piece of paper out. "If this driver's license is any indication, about 1945."

"What's his name?" I asked.

Bob stiffened and hooked his thumbs into his belt loops.

"Booker Lancaster." Victor looked at Bob when he answered.

I repeated the name in my head. It wasn't a name I recognized, but that wasn't surprising. The 1940s were a long time ago.

Bob glanced back over his shoulder at Chris and me. "If you're done taking her statement, go help Harrison."

I didn't have anything else to say. I stared at the body, focusing and unfocusing my eyes. When the body was moved, the green light had moved with it. The tendril still led straight to the body. Whatever dark spell was going on at my house, this old murder case was somehow related.

I backed out of the room and followed Chris back to the lobby.

"Did you get what you were looking for?" He lowered his voice so that Harrison wouldn't overhear.

"I'm not sure. The line led straight to him."

"I guess that means you'll be investigating another murder."

I lowered my head and stepped into him. I pressed my face into his chest, and he wrapped his arms around me and kissed the top of my head.

"If it means anything to you, I have faith you'll catch whoever's responsible. You've got a great track record."

"Even a nearly eighty-year-old case?" I held on to him, my eyes shut, listening to his heartbeat.

"Without a doubt." He kissed my head again.

I could feel his emotions through his clothes. He wasn't lying to me. He had faith and was filled with love and confidence.

"Thank you." I squeezed him tightly then stepped back. I gave him a quick peck on the lips and retreated to my car.

Booker Lancaster. I repeated the name in my head as I pulled out my phone. *Who are you?*

DANI:
Meet me at the Bizzy Bean. I've got news.

One by one, it registered as *read* by the group. The last

one to see it was Heather. She was probably in the middle of cleaning up for the evening. I shoved my phone into my pocket and drove.

I wasn't far from the Bizzy Bean, but the entire group beat me there somehow. *Maybe they were already waiting?* I marched inside, straight back to our usual table, and grabbed a seat at the head of the table. Heather locked the door behind me and joined me a few seconds later.

"Well?" Betty stared at me wide-eyed. "Where did it lead?"

"To a dead body."

The table went still. Agnes gaped. Megan leaned back in her chair, a contemplative look on her face. Heather exhaled sharply.

"Well, I, for one, am not surprised," Sarah said.

Megan chuckled awkwardly. Sometimes, the only way to release tension was to laugh. While I had never done it myself, on some level, I did understand the people who laughed at funerals. The nervous energy had to go somewhere. Some people cried. Some yelled. And some laughed. At times, I wished I were a laugher. Instead, I always had to deal with frustration tears.

"What?" Sarah crossed her arms. "When isn't there a dead body involved? Who was it?"

"Booker Lancaster," I said.

Betty cocked her head to the side. "It sounds vaguely familiar, but I'm having trouble placing it."

"Same." Agnes scrunched up her face.

"He had been in there a while, it looked like. He was sealed up behind a wall. Do you know when they last did work on that building?"

"Decades." Sarah leaned forward.

Betty nodded. "I remember there being a remodel when I was a young child."

"They replaced the carpet in the late nineties," Agnes chimed in.

"But nothing structural," Sarah said.

"His ID was from the forties. He has to have been put in there during the last remodel."

"So..." Heather looked from person to person. "What are we going to do now? The Wardens will be here tomorrow."

"Hide Grace?" Betty grimaced as she said it.

"Or we could just let them do their job." Megan stood.

The Retirees spluttered and talked rapidly over each other. I couldn't make heads or tails out of their objections—but they were clearly objecting. Strenuously.

"We have a lead. Shouldn't we focus on that?" I asked, raising my voice to cut into their conversation.

Heather put her hand over mine. "We don't have time."

"I—"

"I know it's hard, but we have to make a decision now." Heather squeezed my hand.

I closed my eyes. I knew in my gut that Grace was trapped inside her own body, that there was someone to save. She wasn't a lost cause, not yet. But if the Wardens took her, I could lose her forever. Their job was to enforce the three laws of magic. Thou shalt not permanently alter another's mind, body, or spirit without their informed consent. Thou shalt not violate the natural order of things. And thou shalt not make deals with Outsiders to augment your power. While she hadn't made the deal herself, Grace being possessed by an Outsider was too dangerous, and she couldn't be allowed to keep her freedom. They would lock her up and throw away the key.

My breath caught in my throat. "You're right. I just... I wish I had more time."

"The only way to get more time is to hide Grace." Betty glared at Megan, daring her to disagree.

Megan sighed and took a seat at the table. "We could try putting her into a magical sleep."

Agnes sat back and nodded. "That could work."

"But—" Betty held up a finger.

"What's stopping the Wardens from tracking her down with a spell?" Sarah asked.

I chewed on my lip. Tracking a person with magic was hard but not impossible. The only reason I knew Grace's location was the Ring camera at my front door and the motion sensor lights on each corner of the house. Her car was still parked in her usual spot. I had watched her on the Ring camera when she went inside the night I packed my bags and left. Since then, none of the motion sensor lights had gone off to indicate she had left. While I myself hadn't had much luck with tracking a person with magic, that didn't mean someone else more powerful than me couldn't pull it off. The only way I'd ever been able to find someone was by tracking something they were wearing instead. If everything I'd heard about Wardens was right, they probably wouldn't have the same issue. I froze as I mentally went through all the times I'd successfully used tracking magic to find someone again, and I smiled. They might not have the same issue tracking a person, but I had something that might interfere: a magical ring I'd taken from Vincent, a hit man who'd bought it on a magical black market. I'd had to think way outside the box to track him down when he wore it. It might just work and buy me the time I needed to investigate.

"Something tells me you've got an idea." Heather smiled. "Care to share with the class?"

"Vincent's ring."

Megan looked confused. She hadn't been involved in that investigation, so she wouldn't have heard about it. The rest of the table shared my glee.

"It's a magical ring that protects the wearer from tracking magic. It kind of makes them invisible to all attempts to view them from a distance too," I said.

"That's wonderful—" Megan sat up straight in her seat then slumped. "But where are we going to hide her? The

Wardens are going to search all our homes. And they'll know about Heather. They'll notice if there's some sort of magical effect going on at her house."

I grimaced and turned toward the Retirees. "You don't happen to know anyone else in town that we could trust with something like this?"

They immediately began to bicker. I lost track of who was speaking half a second in as they all spoke over each other.

When the argument stopped, Betty was glaring daggers at her two friends. "Am I wrong?"

Sarah raised her hands in surrender.

"Kimberly Jones."

Megan winced and drew back. "If you're going to ask her, it would be best if she didn't know I was involved."

"Why's that?" I asked.

"Bad blood." Megan turned away, hiding her face. "She isn't the forgiving sort."

"Honestly, I think if we ask..." Betty began.

"She wouldn't say yes," Agnes continued where Betty stopped.

Sarah nodded. "Our best bet would be to show up on her doorstep with an unconscious Grace in tow."

Heather's eyes widened, and I spluttered, unsure what to say. *Just show up? Are they nuts?*

Megan sighed and pinched the bridge of her nose. "You're probably right. Her motherly instincts would kick in. She couldn't turn you away."

"I... Are you sure?" I asked.

The four of them nodded. I looked between the Retirees, Megan, and Heather. Heather shrugged and leaned back in her seat. Showing up on someone's doorstep sounded crazy. Kimberly Jones was descended from the same cursed coven as the Retirees, Megan, and me, but she'd made it abundantly clear that she didn't want anything to do with the rest of us when I saw her last. They all knew her better than I did, though.

I sighed. "If this is what's going to keep my daughter safe, then let's do it."

Agnes sighed. "There's another problem."

I threw my hands up. "Of course there is."

Sarah collapsed into her seat. "Right."

"How could we miss it?" Betty shook her head.

"Does someone want to clue me in?" I asked.

"How are we going to prevent the Wardens from using mind-reading magic?" Sarah and Agnes said in unison.

"There has to be a protection spell for that, right?" Heather looked from forlorn face to forlorn face. "Right?"

Silence fell over the table.

It was too much. *How are we supposed to overcome something like this? Am I really going to lose my daughter because I'm not strong enough? Gran... why did you have to hide my heritage from me for so long? If I had time to learn, maybe...* The thought trailed off. There was no maybe. If it wasn't a spell my Retirees knew, it was unlikely my gran knew it either.

I flinched as someone knocked on the glass pane in the front door. I spun around and stared at a guy standing there with a package under one arm and a clipboard in the other. He waved.

Heather stood and scurried to answer it.

"Is there a Dani Williams here?" the man asked.

"Yes?" I stood and slipped out of the plexiglass enclosure. "I'm Dani."

"I've got a package for you." He held out the clipboard for me to sign.

I jotted down my name and took the bundle from him. I turned it over in my hands. It didn't have a return address. It was labeled:

Dani Williams

I cocked an eyebrow and looked up. The man had already walked away. He climbed onto a bike and pedaled down the road. It was a courier service, so the package hadn't gone through the mail.

"What is it?" Heather asked.

I stared at it. The box had a familiar weight. My heart fluttered in my chest. *It can't be.*

"Do you have a knife?" I asked.

Heather grabbed a box cutter from under the counter. My hands trembled as I cut the box open. Inside, wrapped in brown paper, was the last of my Gran's notebooks.

CHAPTER 4

They all gathered around me as I carried the journal to the table. I barely noticed as the plexiglass enclosure door slammed shut behind me. I only had eyes for the book. I stared at it, wide-eyed. I had received the first one when I found out I was a witch. My Gran had left it for me with a letter explaining my heritage. Since then, they had been delivered by a mysterious benefactor. Every single one of them had come at a time of need. And I needed that one right then more than ever.

I flipped the book open and skimmed through the pages hungrily. The book was filled with protection spells. They ranged from protection against physical injury to safeguarding against spiritual possession. None of them was guaranteed. They were almost like vaccines. They increased your natural resistance to things, but none made you impervious. I faltered when I reached the last page. An extra page had been glued to the book. That spell was written in handwriting different from the rest of the book. It looked strikingly similar to the handwriting on the package. It was a spell for protecting against mind reading. And in the bottom-left-hand corner, where it typically said the book was one of seven, the text had been scratched out and replaced with "7 of 8" in the same cursive handwriting as the additional spell.

"Is that what I think it is?" Megan peered over my shoulder.

"Yeah." I slammed the book closed and stood up. I paced around the cat enclosure.

The hairs on my neck and arms stood on end, and the pressure in the back of my head was throbbing. My powers of divination were screaming at me to cast the spell and move on. *But... is this too easy?* Whoever sent it seemed to have a clear idea of what was going on. *Are they spying on me? Why haven't they revealed themselves? What do they want?* I couldn't figure out an answer to that one other than an attempt to help. Every book had been helpful. Every book had been slowly training and leading me.

"I just wish I knew who they were." I collapsed onto my chair. "If they were really just trying to help me, why wouldn't they reveal themselves?"

The Retirees exchanged a look. They claimed not to know who had the books, but I suspected they had an idea. I had one, too, and I didn't like it. I squashed that thought before it had a chance to take hold. I had to focus on Grace. I didn't have time to think about my mother. I opened the book again and reread the spell.

"It's almost like it was tailor-made for this situation," I said.

Megan inched forward in her seat and peered at my face. "Does this mean we're going to do it, then?"

I nodded and slid the book to the center of the table so that they could all read it.

"All right." Megan sighed. "If this is the plan, I'll do it. But only if that's what the group wants."

The Retirees exchanged another look and broke into bickering. I couldn't focus on their words. They spoke over each other but still somehow understood. I cocked my head to the side and stared at them. *But how do they understand?* I unfocused my eyes. They were surrounded by small, barely perceptible iridescent shimmers. Agnes had cast a spell to keep their conversations private. I gritted my teeth.

"What are you fighting about now?" I asked.

Sarah turned to glare at the other two. She crossed her arms over her chest and looked away. Agnes aimed a pointed look at Betty.

I pinched the bridge of my nose. "Just… tell me."

"I feel if the Wardens are going to be treating us like we are a coven, we should be one," Betty grumbled.

Agnes sighed. "I feel like fear is a bad reason to have you two join ours. You can't honestly tell me it isn't informing your thought process."

"And I think fear is a perfect reason to join because, historically, it's why the first one came together," Sarah said.

"It's agreed, then? We'll form a coven?" Betty sounded hopeful.

"Don't we get a vote?" Megan asked.

I stifled a laugh. The Retirees had been in their own circle for so long that it never occurred to them that Megan or I might feel different.

"Well, I… I…" Betty floundered. "I just assumed."

"What does being a coven mean?" I asked.

Agnes cleared her throat. "I don't think there is one straight answer. They are all slightly different."

Sarah picked up where Agnes had left off. "They all have a similar foundation, though. It is a group of witches, usually a minimum of three, that work together."

I raised my eyebrow. "Then aren't we one already?"

Betty shook her head. "When a coven is formed, there is a mystical force that binds them together. They… become more in tune with one another. They can sense each other."

"They know when the other members are in danger," Agnes added.

"And can pull on each other's powers from a distance. Shall we put it to a vote?" Sarah asked.

I glanced over at Megan. She had her eyes averted. Her shoulders were hunched. I leaned over to her. "Are you okay?" I whispered.

She closed her eyes and nodded. "Lost in thought, that's all."

I gave her a quizzical look. "Are you sure?"

"Covens can also be painful when they dissolve," Megan murmured.

I swallowed and looked between her and the Retirees. "Is that true?"

"It can be." Sarah spoke slowly, each word separated by a pause.

My eyes widened. "How painful?"

"It depends on what oaths are sworn at the founding of it," Agnes answered.

Sarah nodded. "We could build into our promises that the coven will last only so long as we are dealing with this issue. That way, when it's done, we can go our separate ways if we want. Or we can revote and form the coven we really want with clearer heads."

"So, do you cast a spell to form one?" Heather asked.

Betty shrugged. "There isn't just one set spell."

"Covens are all unique," Sarah chimed in.

"The group writes it together, so it's personalized. It can be as simple as a declaration to the universe," Agnes said.

"Or a multiday, a-hundred-seventeen-step process involving cleansing rituals and spa days," Betty said. "Typically, the more complicated the ritual, the more accurate the sense of each other becomes."

Agnes squeezed Betty's hand. "We don't just know when each other is in danger."

"We also know how each other feels. And when we concentrate, we know where each other is," Sarah added.

"Always," Betty finished.

I exhaled. That was useful. With the Wardens coming, knowing if the others were in danger would be helpful.

Sarah looked between me and Heather. "While we don't have time to do anything very complicated, it doesn't mean we can't make it special."

I leaned forward in my seat. "Like what?"

"Like we said, every coven is unique," Agnes said.

Betty nodded. "But there are some things that stay consistent."

"It usually involves forming a circle." Sarah ticked things off with her fingers. "Calling on the power in some way. Some circles are very focused on the elements, while others like to call on their ancestors or something like that. And then they always share what their intentions are by joining and swearing some sort of oath to each other."

"The oath is the important part. It's the only part that is absolutely necessary," Betty said.

Agnes settled back into her seat. "It's why I said you just have to say you are one. There's an assumed oath everyone takes when forming a coven."

"And what's that?" I asked.

"Loyalty," Megan murmured.

I shuddered as a shiver went down my spine. Loyalty was at the heart of why we were all cursed. The question was who had broken loyalty first: Meredith, by making her deal with an Outsider, or her coven, by binding her to her house. Either way, we had all ended up cursed. *Is that what Megan meant when she said dissolving a coven can hurt?*

"What *type* of ritual did you use to form yours?" Heather asked.

"One that makes a permanent coven." Betty gave Sarah and Agnes a sidelong look.

Sarah snorted. "Like rituals can't be modified. And you call yourself the expert of transformation."

Betty reddened and looked away. Her curse made casting magic difficult for her. It twisted her intentions, so things never turned out right. It made her scared to use it. I could understand why she was leery to modify anything even if transformation magic was inherent to her.

"I led it last time. Let me write it down, and we can reconfigure it so you two can join it temporarily." Agnes pulled out a notepad from her oversize purse. She scrunched up her nose as she scribbled it down.

When she was done, she ripped the page out and slapped it down on the table. I leaned forward to read it. Her handwriting was not the best. I had to reread it a few times to figure out its meaning.

It was as they'd described: forming a circle in a sacred space, cleansing the area, funneling their magic through each other to bind one another together, sharing their intentions, then chanting their oath before releasing the circle. When Agnes wrote down spells, they almost looked like recipes. At the top was an ingredients list then a step-by-step guide. Her approach to writing spells was very different from my gran's. I almost preferred it. Nothing was more frustrating than making it halfway through a new spell only to discover I needed lavender and had to make a mad dash to the kitchen before I lost focus.

"What sacred space did you use?" I asked.

"Our home," Sarah said.

"It was sacred to us," Betty added.

I chewed on my lip. *What place would be sacred to all of us?* I looked around the Bizzy Bean, from the warm wooden floors to the massive cat tower that took up the rear wall to the artwork on the walls. It was one of the few places I always felt at home. I studied the women around me. They were all at ease in their chairs, even Megan, who rarely made it off her farm. *Can a cafe be a sacred space?*

Once the thought crossed my mind, I couldn't get it out.

Something about the Bizzy Bean being our sacred space felt right. I grabbed the piece of paper from the table and wrote it down. The group looked at the change and nodded.

"If you're doing it here, I almost feel like coffee should be involved. Or hot chocolate. A shared beverage among friends," Heather said.

It was Betty's turn to reach out and grab the piece of paper. She added in a shared drink while they were forming the bond. As the cup went around the table, the spell would pass from person to person.

From there, the piece of paper traveled around the table. Each of us crossed out and added notes here or there until it was a mess. Sarah started a new sheet with all the revisions. Her handwriting was much easier to read. We passed it around the group again and jotted down even more ideas. It was a wordless endeavor. We scratched things out and rewrote them, refining the verbiage of oaths and intentions with each pass. After a while, Sarah had to start the sheet over a third time. That time, none of us had any more changes. It passed from person to person, each of us nodding in agreement, until it ended in Agnes's hands again.

She stared at the page, rereading through it for the third time. "Are we ready, then?"

I swallowed and stared at the spell in her hands. When I first started on my journey, the spell would've been much too complicated for me. But it didn't scare me. The only thing that scared me was failing in our mission.

"All right. Let's do it," I said.

We quickly gathered the supplies. Heather had almost everything on hand, and what she didn't was upstairs in her apartment. We had opted for candles to cleanse the area and mark the boundary of the circle as well as a London Fog for the shared drink. It was delicious, and the lavender would add a touch of protection to the magic.

Heather carried a large mug filled to the brim with the

steaming-hot beverage out from behind the counter. She set it and five smaller cups down on the table. I glanced between her and the cups. My heart ached at the realization that she wouldn't be involved. Heather was my rock. It pained me that I wouldn't have the same knowledge of her safety that I would the others.

My head swiveled between her and the other women, tears forming at the corners of my eyes.

"Are you okay?" Megan asked.

I nodded but couldn't keep the tears from forming. It was stupid. Heather would still be my best friend.

"You don't look all right." Megan patted my shoulder. "What's wrong?"

"The stress must be getting to me. I don't know why I'm so upset." I wiped my eyes. "I just… I wish Heather could join the coven with us."

"I don't see why she can't," Megan said.

My eyes widened. "She can? But she isn't a witch."

"Everyone has magical energy inside," Agnes said.

Betty stepped up next to me and placed a hand on my shoulder. "It's what makes us human."

"But only those descended from witches can access the power and manipulate it to cast spells," Sarah finished.

"If she joins the coven, would she be become a witch?" I asked.

Megan shook her head. "You would both be able to sense each other and know when each other is in danger. But she would still be Heather. She would still be… normal."

Being able to sense when she was in danger meant I would have one less thing to worry about when I tried to figure out how to save Grace. If the Wardens hurt her, I would know. I spun toward Heather. "Do you want to join our coven?"

Heather pulled me into a hug. "With all my heart."

I squeezed her and stepped back. "Then go get one more cup."

Heather scampered away to get another. I was rereading the spell one last time when she returned with it. She set it down on the table. Her hands shook, and she shoved them under her elbows as she crossed her arms over her chest.

I exhaled slowly, trying to steady myself. Like Heather, my fingers were trembling. We'd been working together for so long that forming a coven did seem like the natural next step. But at the same time, I understood where Agnes was coming from. Fear of losing my daughter was forcing the decision.

"Are you ready?" I asked.

The group nodded. We each grabbed a lighter from the pile on the table and formed ourselves into a circle. Agnes picked up the stack of tea lights from the table. She started with Betty. An iridescent shimmer floated from her mouth to the candle and settled over it. She handed it to Betty. One by one, she walked around the circle, doing the same action with Sarah, Megan, Heather, and finally me. She joined the circle in the opening we had left her. She exhaled over her handle, a shimmer settling over the candle in her hand. The candles flashed, and strings of light streamed between them.

Agnes held up her lighter, and the rest of us in the circle followed suit. In unison, we lit our candles and raised them overhead, turned, and deposited the candles on the floor behind us. The motes of light swirled through the space, creating a globe of light around us. My breath shook as I turned back toward the group. It was beautiful.

Agnes glided into the center of the circle. She picked up the mug filled with the London Fog and poured it into the smaller empty cups. She grabbed the first one and carried it to Betty. "I ask you, what is your intention behind temporarily expanding this coven?"

"I, Betty Taylor, temporarily expand the coven to fulfill my promise to protect the Williams line."

She repeated the process with the others. The shimmering light swam around us and pulsed and swirled faster and faster with each promise.

"I, Sarah Hill, temporarily expand the coven in the hope that together, we can make a brighter future."

"I, Megan Miller, join the coven in the hope of repairing that which was broken."

As Megan accepted the cup, Agnes bowed her head and murmured, "I welcome you to the coven with an open mind and an open heart."

"I, Heather Bellerose, join the coven to support my found family in their trials and tribulations."

My turn finally came. I took the cup from Agnes. The lights were so bright that I could barely see the others.

"I ask you, what is your intention behind joining this coven?"

"I, Dani Williams, join this coven in the hopes that we may rescue my daughter from the Outsider and break the curse placed on most of our families by Meredith Walker."

Agnes returned to the center of the circle and picked up the last cup on the table. She took her spot next to me in the circle.

Once she was in place, in unison, the rest of us asked the question: "We ask you, what is your intention behind temporarily expanding this coven?"

"I, Agnes Price, join it to offer support to those I hold dear in these trying times, in the memory of a departed friend."

"We welcome you to the coven with open minds and open hearts," the group said together.

Agnes held the small mug aloft. We all followed suit then drank the tea together. It was delicious. I drank it in three large mouthfuls.

I didn't think it was possible, but the room became even brighter. Motes of light streamed out of me in a whirlwind. My motes of light joined the shimmering haze created by Agnes. It was joined by tiny flames from Sarah, globes of strangely formed pearls from Betty, and translucent flower petals from Megan. The light seemed to be pulled out of me. I didn't know if I could have stopped even if I tried. I didn't have to focus on maintaining it. I just had to focus on finishing it before the torrent of magic overwhelmed me and bled me dry.

Agnes reached out to the side and grasped onto me. I held my hand out for Heather's waiting hand. I clutched onto them. Between gasps, I joined the group as they intoned the oath we'd decided upon. "On this day, I swear upon all that I love that I will work with this coven until Grace Lee has been saved from the Outsider influencing her mind and body."

I closed my eyes as the light flashed once more then vanished.

It worked.

I could feel them in my mind. The connection wasn't like what I shared with Charlie, but it was similar. I could sense them—not where they were or what they were feeling, but I could sense their existence. I gasped as I examined the new sensation. Each one of them felt different. Some were bigger than others. I almost seemed to be getting an impression of their power. Sarah was a giant in my mind, while Heather was small, like a delicate flower. It was disorientating for a second.

"I can feel you," I whispered.

Heather squeezed my hand. "I can too. It's amazing."

I opened my eyes and looked at her. She smiled.

Betty grabbed her candle from the floor and blew it out. "All right, then. Now that's out of the way. Let's get the protection against mind-reading spells in place and then go put Grace to sleep."

CHAPTER 5

Before we left, I rechecked the Ring door camera. In the porch light, I could still see Grace's car parked in her usual spot. My nerves were shot, and I couldn't stop my hands from shaking when I got behind the wheel, so I let Heather take the lead. Her presence was calming, so by the time we parked in front of my house, I was almost back in control of myself. Almost. I probably would have been if my home weren't so creepy. I swallowed a lump in my throat as I stared up at it from the passenger seat. Nothing was obviously wrong. The house looked normal. But a heaviness weighed down the air, like a spiritual oil slick. I felt mentally slimy as I studied the darkened windows.

Grace's car was parked where I'd seen it on the camera. If her car was there, there was a good chance she was too. Things were far enough apart out there that going into town or visiting with a neighbor was outside a comfortable walking distance.

I cleared my throat. "I'm ready."

Heather turned off her engine, and we climbed out together. We walked to the front of the car, and she held my hand as we walked toward the house. The Retirees met us at the base of the stairs leading up to the porch. They fell into formation after me as I shuffled up the stairs. I couldn't force any confidence into my walk. My shoulders were hunched so high that they almost rubbed against the bottoms of my ears.

The living room was quiet as I pushed the front door open. I stepped cautiously into the room. Everything still looked normal, from the couch against the far wall, to the family photo of me, Gran, and my mom over the fireplace from when I was pregnant with Grace, to the assortment of knickknacks along the floating shelves, which I still hadn't brought myself to get rid of. It was exactly like my Gran had decorated, with a few newer touches from me and Grace.

I glanced behind me at the rest of the coven. They followed me into the room, lingering by the front door as I moved farther into the house. Grace was my daughter, so I was taking the lead. I glanced into the kitchen and froze. Sitting with her back to me, staring out the window into the side yard, was Grace.

"You haven't been home in a few days." Grace's voice was flat, devoid of any warmth. She turned in her seat and stared at me with her dark-brown eyes.

Panic flooded my brain. I floundered for a response. *Is this her? How far gone is she?* I forced a smile onto my face. "Sorry, sweetie. It's been kind of a whirlwind week."

Grace stood. "I heard you found another body."

My heart raced, beating faster. Adrenaline surged through me. *She hasn't left the house. How did she hear that?* Standing still took everything I had. The pressure in the back of my head was pulsing.

"I did," I croaked.

Grace took a step forward. "It must have been heart-breaking for Beau's family when he disappeared."

I cocked my head to the side. *Beau? Who's Beau?*

"Oops." Grace smiled and covered her mouth, but the

smile didn't reach her eyes. "I guess I wouldn't know what his nickname is, would I?"

Green sparkles erupted from her and flew around the room. Cutlery from the dish rack rose into the air and spun until they faced me with the pointy ends. I threw myself to one side as the knives sailed through the air toward me.

Agnes darted forward and held her hands up, screaming wordlessly. The knives slowed and fell to the ground. I rolled past the kitchen into the hallway, crouched next to the doorway, and peeked inside.

"Traitors!" Grace bellowed.

The way she said it sent shivers down my spine. It was the exact same way Meredith had yelled it at her coven when they came to stop her. My vision narrowed. *Are we too late?*

Betty and Sarah joined Agnes in the middle of the room. Heather hugged the wall closest to the front door, and Megan stood opposite me, just out of sight of Grace in the kitchen.

"Hurry!" Betty held out her hand to Agnes.

I stood and grabbed Agnes's other hand. The moon wasn't full, so Sarah would be of limited help. We had to contain Grace so that Megan could work her magic on her. I funneled my power into Agnes as she muttered the words to a spell under her breath.

The silverware rattled on the floor as Grace stalked toward us. As she stepped into the doorway, Agnes loosed her spell. Wind swirled through the house and picked Grace up. It held her in the air, wrapping her arms around her body. Grace thrashed, causing her to slowly spin in midair. I kept funneling my power into Agnes. My motes of soft golden light swirled among her iridescent waves. Betty's irregular-size pearls mingled in the air. Everything combined into a seething spiral of lights.

Megan stepped out from her hiding place and reached into the tornado. Her magic looked like red flower petals.

They streamed through the chaos and settled over Grace's eyes and ears.

Grace stilled and stared at me. The hate in her eyes vanished, replaced by terror. Her jaw quivered as she held my gaze. "Mommy? What... No... I'm so sorry."

The red petals sank into her skin, and Grace went limp in the air. We released the spell, and she fell to the ground. I rushed forward and pulled her onto my lap.

"Grace?" I stroked her hair. "That was her that said that, right? You heard it?" I looked up at the Retirees as they surrounded us.

Betty nodded.

"There's still hope." Sarah squeezed my shoulder.

I choked back a sob. *We made it in time. She's still in there.* The Wardens hadn't arrived yet. We could still hide her while we figured things out. They weren't going to take her away from me—not yet anyway. I fumbled with the magical ring that would protect her from tracking magic and shoved it onto her finger. I tried to pick her up on my own, but even with all the extra strength training sessions I had taken up, I still struggled because lifting a person was unwieldy. I could handle the heaviness, but she was dead weight, so she did nothing to make carrying her easier.

Heather darted over and grabbed her other side. Together, we lifted her from the floor and carried her out of the house to Betty's truck.

Megan ran ahead of us and climbed into the back seat. "I'll monitor her from back here, just in case."

I nodded and laid my daughter across the back seat, with her head in Megan's lap. I stared at her numbly. She looked so peaceful sleeping. It was a deep, deep sleep. Watching the petals moving around under her eyelids was odd. "Do you know what she's dreaming about?"

"If I cast the spell right? Nothing," Megan said.

I nodded and closed the door. I walked to Heather's car in

a daze. Nothing felt real. My daughter had attacked me. *But it wasn't really her. Grace wouldn't do that if she were in control of her own body.*

We backed out of the driveway. Heather pulled to the side so that the Retirees could lead the way again. She followed them into town, through the downtown area, and out the other side, where the newest suburbs had sprung up a few years back. We came to a stop outside a one-story rambler-style house at the end of a cul-de-sac, with a large four-car garage on one side. The front walkway cut across the yard, perpendicular to the road.

I scrambled out of Heather's car and strode to the side of Betty's truck. Grace was still unconscious in the back seat. Heather helped me lift Grace out.

Megan ducked her head and looked away from me, out the side window. "I think I'll wait in the truck."

"What? But what if—"

Betty cut me off. "Heather should probably wait too. We wouldn't want to start on the wrong foot. And outing her to someone else, especially a nonwitch, would sour the whole thing."

"Aren't we already starting on the wrong foot?" I asked.

Betty turned on her heel and marched up the driveway. "Well, there's the wrong foot. And then there's the wrong, wrong foot."

I exchanged a look with Heather. She shrugged and climbed into the truck next to Megan. Sarah and Agnes took her place on the other side of Grace, and together, we shuffled up the driveway toward Kimberly's house.

As we turned onto the walkway, Betty pounded on the front door. "Kim! Kim, we need you!" Betty yelled.

Warm light fell onto Betty as the front door flew open. "Whatever you're here for, I'm not interested," Kimberly said from inside the house.

"Kimberly, please. I need your help." I stumbled forward, trying to get Grace in sight of the front door.

Kimberly leaned on her forearm crutches as she stepped out onto the concrete step in front of her home. "What did I tell you—" She faltered as her eyes landed on Grace. "What is this?"

"The Wardens are coming. They're going to take her away. Please, you have to help me," I said.

Kimberly's mouth opened and closed. She looked between me, my daughter, and Betty standing on her doorstep. She shook her head and stepped back into her house. "I don't need to do anything."

I took the last few steps to her front door and shoved my foot in between the door and the frame before she could close it. "I just need a bit more time to figure out how to save her. Please, Kimberly."

"Who is she? And save her from what?" Kimberly asked from behind the door. She peered out at me, only one eye visible through the crack.

"She's my daughter. Her name is Grace. She was infected by something when we went into Meredith—" I winced as she tried to force the door closed on my foot. "I just… I need a few days. That's all. Please. She's the only family I have left. Please. I can't lose her too."

"Mom." The voice was muffled and coming from someplace inside the house. "It's the right thing to do."

"Lindsey—"

"What if it was me?"

The pressure on my foot subsided. A second later, Kimberly opened the door. Behind her, standing in the hallway, was a blond girl, maybe fifteen years old, wearing an oversize basketball jersey.

Kimberly glared at me. "A few days. I'll hold you to it."

"Thank you, thank you, thank you." I cried as we carried Grace inside.

We followed Kimberly to a guest bedroom at the back of the house. I laid Grace gently on the bed and stepped back as Kimberly looked her over.

She snorted. "You can tell Megan that she should stop being a coward and come face me."

"Megan?" Betty feigned ignorance. "I haven't—"

Kimberly raised an eyebrow. "Do you really think I wouldn't recognize her magic?"

The Retirees hung their heads and filtered out of the room.

I lingered and watched as Kimberly cast a second sleep spell over Grace. Then she followed the Retirees out into the living room. I stared down at my daughter. Her face was relaxed. All the worry lines had faded. I kissed her gently on her forehead. "Don't worry, sweetie. Your momma's coming for you."

I followed the sound of voices to the living room.

"And I expect one of you to check in on us at least once a day. You've got it? I'll give you a week. No more. And if you haven't come to get her by then, I'll call the Wardens myself."

A week? I wavered in the doorway. *Can I figure it out in a week? It took over a day to find the first clue.*

"It's a deal." Betty held out her hand.

They shook, and Kimberly showed us to the door. The Retirees exhaled and slouched as it closed behind us.

"What did Megan do to her?" I asked.

Agnes shrugged. "We don't know."

"Not the specifics anyway," Betty said.

"They used to be really good friends. But they had a falling out almost twenty years ago." Sarah glanced back at the house as we shuffled down the walkway.

Agnes sighed. "Overnight, Kim cut us all out. Megan retreated to her family farm."

"Her mom wouldn't tell us. Said it was between the girls," Sarah said.

"But whatever it was, it had to be really bad. Because that's when Kim had to start using her crutches," Betty finished.

I stared back at the house. I had a week to figure things out, or the Wardens would take my daughter. As much as I wanted to fix whatever bad blood was going on between Megan and Kimberly, I didn't have time for that right then. I gritted my teeth and clenched my hands into fists as I climbed into Heather's car. She joined me a minute later, and we drove away in silence.

I prayed that Chris wouldn't mind helping with more investigation. After I came clean to him about being a witch, he'd been a lot more understanding of my need to investigate. But I didn't want to make him feel like I was using him for his access to information, not when things were going so well. But I wasn't sure where to start with an almost-eighty-year-old case, especially with such a small window to solve it. I needed his help.

CHAPTER 6

At almost ten o'clock at night, I got back to Chris's townhome. Most of the lights were out. He'd left the entryway light on and had gone up to bed. I joined him but couldn't sleep, even with Charlie curled up and purring in my arms. For three hours of tossing and turning, my mind replayed that moment Grace looked at me, her eyes pleading, and called me Mommy. She hadn't called me that in years. She'd grown out of it. But I understood the desire to return to the safety of childhood. She just wanted to be safe, to be my little girl again. And instead, she was unconscious. My stomach was queasy. And no matter how long I lay there in the dark with my eyes closed, I couldn't get my mind to turn off and go to sleep.

I slipped out of bed and tiptoed out of the room with Charlie at my heels. I trailed my fingers along the wall as I made my way down to the kitchen in the dim light. I flicked on the light switch and moved around the kitchen, searching through the various cupboards until I found everything I was looking for. I'd been there only a few days, and I still wasn't used to the layout. I needed a minute to collect the kettle, a mug, and the chamomile tea I'd spotted at the back of a cabinet on my first day there.

I rested with my butt against the counter until the kettle hissed then quickly went through the motions to make myself a cup of tea. With a mug in hand, I stepped into the darkened living room and flipped on the light. I froze as my eyes landed on a woman sitting in a chair in the corner.

The word *striking* didn't do the woman justice. She was unusual looking. She had long white hair that flowed in waves around her shoulders. Her features had a timeless quality. I couldn't tell if she was young or old. She could have been sixty or twenty-six. It was impossible to tell. She held my gaze. I couldn't move or blink. I could just stare into her eyes and wonder at the beauty of them. One eye was a vivid purple and the other a stormy gray.

An inky darkness slid across the floor toward me. I opened my mouth to scream, but the sound died in my throat as the darkness touched my foot. It locked me in place. I stood there, eyes wide and mouth open, almost like I was staring at her through a tunnel. Everything around us faded into the background until it was just me and her eyes. Inside my head, I screamed. Through my bond with Charlie, I could feel him screaming too. Neither of us could move. The mug of tea slipped from my frozen fingers and crashed to the floor, the mug breaking into pieces at my feet.

The woman smiled. "You must be Danielle Williams. Daughter of Lorelai Williams. And granddaughter to Melinda Williams. Good witches. It would be a shame if the track record of keeping out of trouble were to end with you."

My eyes watered. I couldn't look away. *How can she be smiling?*

"My name is Delaney Thornhill. My friends call me Laney. I am hoping that maybe we can still be friends. I am here, after all, to help you."

The darkness receded enough for me to blink and swallow. I still couldn't speak.

"My associate will be arriving soon, and I wanted to have the opportunity to talk before she got here. She can be… so unreasonable at times."

Every muscle in my body tensed. If she was the reasonable one, I wasn't sure I wanted to meet her associate.

"So I am going to ask you a few questions. And we are going to have a nice, polite conversation. I'll let you move your head so you can nod if you understand." She lifted her finger, and the darkness pulled back even further.

I couldn't open my mouth, but I could move my head up and down. I did so.

"Good. It's so nice to see that you're going to cooperate. Let us begin with an easy question. Where is Grace?"

Something went off in my head. It was loud and blaring, like a fire alarm. My eyes widened a fraction. It was the sound I would hear if someone tried to read my thoughts. Since I knew she was there, I could feel her prying at the edges of my mind.

Delaney sighed. "Things are so much easier if you don't fight. Not just for me but for you too."

Charlie floated across the room to her. She snatched him out of the air and set him on her lap. It was awkward. He stood like he was still on solid ground as she petted him. He teetered back and forth with each motion, his legs unbending.

"I'll ask you again: Where is Grace?" Delaney's voice took on a singsong quality.

I fought the urge to answer her. I swallowed again as she gave me back control of my mouth. "I'm not home to check. But given the time of night, I would assume in bed."

Delaney narrowed her eyes as the fire alarm in my mind sounded again. She pursed her lips and continued to pet Charlie. "We are not the enemy."

You could have fooled me. I glared at her.

"We are here to help. Don't you want your daughter to be safe?" Her voice shifted in tone. It took on a caring quality.

The darkness played around my feet. I wanted so badly to believe her. Something inside me whispered that she was there for my benefit. That was drowned out by the rest of me screaming to fight.

"I do want her to be safe," I said. *Not with you.*

"Good." Delaney slid her hand down Charlie's back again then placed him gently on the ground before rising to her feet.

Charlie bolted and threw himself at me. The hold on my muscles relaxed half a second before he reached me. I scooped him up into my arms and pressed my face into his fur.

"I will be back with my associate. I pray for your sake that you will be more forthcoming with her." She glided toward the door, her long white hair swaying behind her. "I would, of course, suggest not leaving town. Fleeing would be seen as an admission of guilt."

My heart thundered in my chest as she opened the front door and stepped out into the darkened street.

"Oh, and Miss Williams?"

"Yes?" I croaked.

"Please don't tell any of your coven members about our… little conversation." Dark tendrils flowed toward me from the doorway.

I swallowed as the darkness wrapped its way up my legs. "I won't."

With those words, something snapped into place. I could feel it in there like a wall inside my head. It felt like I'd just made a promise I couldn't break.

"Good." She shut the door behind herself.

I stood there for a long time after the door closed, my

face pressed into Charlie's fur. My whole body shook. *How are we supposed to stand up to someone like that?*

After ten minutes, I calmed myself. I hugged Charlie to my chest as I locked the front door and fled to the bedroom, my mug of chamomile tea forgotten on the floor.

CHAPTER 7

I sat there all night, Charlie held to my chest, and stared blankly forward. Every noise made me jump. I peered into every dark corner, half expecting Delaney to materialize in the room with me. As the sun crested the horizon and dawn broke, I finally relaxed enough to close my eyes and got half an hour of sleep before my alarm went off. I groaned and rolled over to turn it off.

Chris was half-asleep next to me. He pulled me in and breathed in my scent as he rested his head on top of mine. "Five more minutes," he said.

I hit the snooze button and relaxed into his arms. The last night had been terrifying, but something about the daylight made it easier to face. Delaney had wanted to scare me. If she could have forced an answer, she would have. She had relied on theatrics for a reason. *Didn't she?* I squeezed my eyes shut. I had to focus on things I could affect. Wardens were outside of my control. I had to focus on the investigation.

When the alarm sounded again, we climbed out of bed. We took turns in the shower then went downstairs for breakfast.

Chris faltered at the base of the stairs. The broken mug

was still sitting in the middle of the room. "What happened here?"

I hugged my arms to my body. *Chris isn't a member of my coven. I can still tell him.* I probed at the wall. I'd found a chink in the promise. "A midnight Warden visit."

He exhaled sharply and sprang into motion. He checked all the windows and doors first, making sure they were locked, then he cleaned up the mess. While he moved, he asked questions. "Who are the Wardens? I think you said something about them being like the police?"

"They are."

He glanced at me. "Then shouldn't you be happy about them being here to help?"

I shook my head. "They're not here to protect and serve. At least not on the individual level. Think of them more like… the KGB. They are here to enforce their own twisted view of the greater good."

He pulled me into a hug and guided me to a table in the kitchen nook to sit down. "So, what are you going to do?"

I picked at my cuticles. "I'm not sure where to start. But I think I need to solve Booker Lancaster's murder."

Chris nodded and collected the ingredients for breakfast: bacon, eggs, and potatoes. "Because the green tendril thing went straight to his body?"

"Yeah." When Charlie leaped up next to me and head-butted my arm, I pulled him onto my lap. "It can't be a coincidence. It went from my house to his body. What's the chance of that? I think if I can figure it out, I can save Grace and… and the Wardens will just have to go home empty-handed."

"Do you think that's likely? If they really are like the KGB, I doubt they go home empty-handed very often."

I grimaced. I didn't want to think about them taking in an innocent girl. *Grace is going to be okay. She has to be.* "Let a girl dream, okay?"

He chopped the potatoes and tossed them into a pan with some hot oil and herbs. "Booker's niece took a red-eye into Seattle last night."

My head snapped up. "He has family in town?"

He nodded. "Imani Jackson. She came in from Georgia. When Bob called her, she ordered the ticket while they were still on the phone."

I stood. "I need to talk to her."

"She has a meeting with Victor in half an hour." He slid a cup of coffee in front of me. "Eat breakfast first, and you can bump into her when she's done talking to him."

I stood up and wrapped my arms around his neck. I raised myself up on my tippy-toes and kissed him. "You are so good to me."

He kissed me back. "You're worth it."

I settled into my seat and followed him with my eyes as he cooked. He somehow made me feel like the luckiest girl in the world. Even as my life was falling down around me, at least I had that.

The funeral home Victor operated out of was in the middle of a suburban neighborhood. The building looked almost like any of the other two-story Craftsman on the block, but it had an unusual chimney stack at the back of the home, and a wooden sign sat in the yard for the business. I parked across the street, behind a rental car, and watched the front door.

Five minutes after I arrived, Victor opened the front door, and a woman stepped out onto the porch. I climbed out of my car and walked toward them as they spoke to each other in hushed tones.

The woman held herself tall. She wore black slacks and an emerald jewel-toned blouse with a red peacoat over it.

Her black hair was in a ponytail, its tight curls swaying behind her head as she nodded.

Victor glanced at me as I approached. He was back to his usual regency-style clothing. His high-necked coat hung around him, silver embroidery detailing the trim. He smiled, an almost expectant look on his face. "Imani, this is Dani, a good friend of mine."

I held out my hand. "Nice to meet you."

Imani's skin was cool to the touch. Her handshake was strong, and she held my gaze as she sized me up.

"You know what? It's chilly out. Do you want to grab a quick cup of coffee before you hit the road?" Victor turned to Imani. "I promise it will be worth your while."

Imani raised an eyebrow and glanced between the two of us, a bemused expression on her face. "Okay. A coffee."

I followed them inside. Victor led us to a sitting room off the main foyer. Compared to Victor, everything in there was drab. It was all muted tones and off-whites. It was the most neutral room I had ever stepped into.

"Dani has been really helpful at ferreting out the truth in hard-to-solve cases," Victor said. "How do you take your coffee?"

"Two sugars, no cream," Imani said.

I took a seat as Victor walked out of the room. Imani stood and stared at me before taking a seat in a stiff-backed chair next to me. "Are you some sort of psychic?"

"Have you had a bad experience with them or something?" I leaned against the plush armrest of the couch and let a finger slide across the armrest of her chair. I could pick up the emotional resonance someone left behind on an object. If someone was still touching it, I could get a nearly real-time read on their emotional state. It wasn't an exact science, but it was close. My chest tightened, and my neck stiffened as her arm came into contact with the seat. She had a strong contempt for psychics. I smiled, trying to seem sympathetic.

She snorted. "They fleeced my mother when her dementia set in. She was so focused on finding Beau that she fell for their tricks over and over again."

A bitter taste formed in the back of my mouth. I tried to swallow it, my throat becoming sore. "Luckily for you, I'm not one."

"Oh?"

"I'm a claims adjuster," I said.

She blinked.

"I was there when they found him." I shifted in my seat, trying to maintain contact with her chair without looking awkward. "It may sound odd, but in my line of work, you end up getting called out to a lot of crime scenes. After looking at a lot of them over the years, I've gotten good at picking things up that others miss."

"Victor says you're... good at this?" Imani raised an eyebrow. Her distrust was slowly shifting toward curiosity.

"I've helped solve a few cases."

Victor swept into the room, his long coat flaring around his legs as he walked. He had a metal serving tray in hand, with cute white porcelain teacups perched on it. He set the tray down on a side table and bowed out of the room.

Imani reached for her coffee cup. She sniffed at it first and took a tentative sip. When she lifted the cup to take a second sip, I mumbled a relaxation spell under my breath. Golden motes of light swirled out of my mouth and streamed straight to her cup. The lights settled over the liquid, and when she took a third sip, the light flowed from the coffee into her skin. She took on a subtle glow. Once again, I was glad only witches could see magical energies. It made casting spells like that feasible in public.

"Are you open to talking to me about your uncle?" I asked.

Imani studied her coffee before responding. "I feel like I know him, but I never actually met Beau. My mother talked about him a lot, especially at the end. In her final days, she felt like he had just gone missing. She passed last year."

My eyes watered. I had kept my fingertips on the edge of her chair. She was filled with so much sorrow that thinking straight became hard.

I cleared my throat. "My condolences for your loss."

She nodded and set the teacup down. She folded her hands in her lap and turned her head away from me to stare out the bay window at the street. "When Sheriff Wright called about the body, I hopped on the first flight out of Georgia. My mom didn't get to have answers, but I like to think she's still watching, that she still needs them, you know?"

I softened my voice and held myself still in my seat so I wouldn't spook her. "Do you remember what she said about his disappearance?"

"She was a wreck about it. Beau was the primary bread-winner for the family. He took his obligations seriously. She knew something had happened, but she didn't know what. Mom did everything she could think of to try to find him. She filed a missing person report. Put up posters. She canvassed the neighborhood with those who were willing to help. She even put out a classified ad."

"Did anyone come forward with information?" I asked.

Imani shook her head. "No one cared about a missing Black man. Not back then. Not when the Black man had the audacity to become engaged to a white woman. Not a single person looked." Imani scoffed. "The sheriff at the time told my mom to stop bothering the good townsfolk. No one helped. And after my family lost their house, she had to give up her search and move someplace… friendlier. She hung on here as long as she could, but after a few years of nothing, she took off for New York."

"A white woman?" My heart skipped a beat. "Do you know where she ended up?"

"Meredith left town a few months later. My mom never heard from her again."

A cold sensation settled into my gut. The way Grace had spoken during our confrontation, I sensed a connection, but knowing something in your heart was different from knowing something with your mind too. "What was her last name?"

"Walker."

I swallowed. "Do you know if Beau had any fights or altercations with anyone in the days or weeks leading up to his disappearance?"

"My mom said he got into a fight with Mac Turner. They were army buddies. But no one ever looked into it, and Mac refused to talk to her. He told her to just let it be."

I filed his name away. The subtle glow around her skin was fading. "Would you mind giving me your number? In case I think of any more questions?"

"Are you really serious about finding out what happened to my uncle?" she asked.

I held her eyes. I filled my gaze with as much sincerity as I could muster and nodded.

She pulled out a business card and handed it to me. She was a registered nurse.

I pocketed it and stood before the relaxation spell faded. "Thank you for your time."

I glanced back at her before leaving the room. She sat there, staring out the window, her coffee forgotten in front of her. I could imagine what she was going through. We'd found him a year too late for her mom to have answers. I had to find them, not just for me and Grace but for her too. No one deserved to sit with the unknown like that.

I held back my tears until I got to my car. I drove a few blocks away and parked under a large aspen tree before I let myself fully break down. Interviewing grieving people was never easy. It had only gotten harder after my witch powers came in and I could feel how they felt. Imani's mother had lived a lifetime not knowing why her brother Beau had left her. A family member disappearing like that hit a bit too close to home for me. My mother had vanished on me. The difference was I knew my mother had abandoned me. Imani's mom had nothing.

After a few minutes, I got myself together. I blotted the tears from my eyes, blew my nose, and got on with it.

CHAPTER 8

I drove mindlessly through downtown as I mulled over the possibilities. I had a name, but I didn't really know much about Beau Lancaster or his military buddy, Mac. Normally, I would look them up on social media and prowl through their profiles to understand who they were. But that wasn't an option in that case, at least for Beau. He'd died decades before social media was a thing. *Then what?* I chewed on my lip. The Retirees hadn't remembered who Beau was when I gave them the name the night before. The only other person I could think of was Willow. She was a town history buff.

I drove to the Slice of Life Diner to find her. Spots were open right outside. I parked and headed in. My stomach rumbled as the scent of bacon mixed with brown sugar and apples filled my nose. The diner was largely empty that time of day. The breakfast rush had filtered out, and the lunch rush wouldn't start for another half an hour at least. Willow and Abby were seated behind the counter, their heads inclined toward each other, as they handed a notebook back and forth. After Abby lost her lease at the bistro, she'd been operating out of Willow's kitchen at the diner instead.

Abby and Willow turned toward me as I approached the

counter. They slid the notebook out of sight. I cocked an eyebrow as I came to a stop. Their being so secretive wasn't normal.

"What can we get you?" Willow asked. She pushed her red-rimmed glasses up her nose and fidgeted with her flowing paisley maxi dress.

"What are you guys up to?" I asked.

"Nothing." Abby shoved the notebook farther under the counter.

"We're planning an expansion," Willow blurted.

Abby turned to Willow, her mouth agape. "We weren't supposed to tell anyone yet," she hissed between her teeth.

"I take it that working together has been going well, then?" I asked.

They both nodded and gushed over how much better their cooking had become. While I didn't want to think about eating, I couldn't help my mouth watering. They were both very talented chefs.

"But you can't tell anyone." Willow pleaded with her eyes.

I held my hands up and mimed zipping my mouth shut and throwing away the key. "Your secret's safe with me."

Willow relaxed into her seat.

Abby covered her mouth, trying not to giggle. "So… what will it be?"

"Apple pie milkshake and a bacon cheeseburger," I said.

Abby jotted that down and stood to slide the slip of paper to the line cook waiting in the kitchen. "It'll be right out. Take a seat."

"Actually…" I leaned against the counter. "I was hoping to talk to Willow about something. When you get a chance, could you stop by my table?"

Willow nodded.

I grabbed my order number card and claimed the booth in the back corner. The Slice of Life Diner was decorated with photos and memorabilia from the town's history.

Willow had recently redone the displays, and each section was dedicated to important events from the town's history. The back corner was dedicated to the founding of Point Pleasant. The photos were black-and-white and grainy. All the men wore suits, and the women had on large, voluminous skirts and high-necked bodices.

After a few minutes, Willow carried the tray of food to my table. Abby trailed behind her, and they slid into the booth opposite me.

The tray was filled. In addition to the milkshake and burger, they'd also heaped on a mound of fries with a side of brown gravy and a slice of triple chocolate cake. I took a bite of the burger first. It was perfectly cooked, and the bacon was crisp. Any other day, I would've been ecstatic about the food. But even though I was ravenous, my usual comfort foods were like ash in my mouth.

Willow leaned forward. "So, what did you need?"

"Did you hear about what happened at the old sheriff's station?" I asked.

"They found a body in the wall," Willow said.

"I'm trying to figure out what happened to him." I dunked a fry into the gravy.

Neither one of them looked surprised.

"How can we help?" Willow asked.

"I know you have a lot of photos from the forties. I was wondering if you might know something about him or have photos of him."

"Maybe? I know the current history better. Getting people to share stories from back then is harder because there aren't as many residents who were around back then."

I sighed. "That's what I was worried about."

"What was his name?" Abby asked.

"Booker Lancaster. But it sounds like he went by Beau. I have the beginnings of a lead. I know he got into a fight with someone named Mac Turner before he disappeared."

"I don't recognize the names. But you can take a look through my boxes of photos if you want."

"How many boxes are there?"

Willow blushed. "From the 1940s? I think I only have seventeen banker boxes."

I spluttered on my water. *Seventeen banker boxes? That would take days to go through.* "No wonder you can change out the displays so often. How on earth do you keep it all straight?"

"She has help," Abby said.

Willow nodded. "I'm friends with the curator at the local historical society. I loan her some of my collection on occasion, and she helps me make heads or tails of my donations."

"There's a historical society?" I raised an eyebrow. Point Pleasant wasn't exactly a large town.

"Of course!" Willow beamed. "This town has a fun history. The historical society has an even bigger collection than I do. While I just have more photos, they have copies of the local newspaper going back to its first ever publication."

I grimaced. I had a mental image of a tower of boxes looming over me.

"It's all on microfiche. And they have a robust catalogue to help narrow things down. The curator is an absolute sweetheart. Her name's Donna." Willow pulled out her order pad to write. "When you stop by, you should tell her Willow sent you."

She ripped the piece of paper off and handed it to me. I stared down at an address. It was a few blocks away. I scrunched up my face. I'd driven through that neighborhood hundreds of times. I didn't remember seeing a historical society there, but I hadn't exactly been looking. I held up the piece of paper. "Thanks a million, Willow."

The front door opened as the first of the lunch rush arrived. They climbed out of the booth, leaving me to finish eating my food. I didn't know how much magic I would need to use that day, so staying fueled up would be best. Magic burned more calories than an intense gym workout. While I had too much food for one person, I shoveled as much of it away as I could. When I couldn't eat any more, I slipped out of the booth and headed out to go find the historical society.

I stared up at the building. I didn't know how I'd missed it. The structure was massive. It was a four-story brick building, and the first story was closer to two stories tall. The metal-studded double doors towered over me, and carved in big block letters across the main entrance were the words *Point Pleasant Historical Society*. I swallowed and stepped inside.

Silence engulfed me. The sound of my heart beating filled my ears as I padded across the large foyer toward the front desk. A woman sat behind the counter, her head lowered, as she flipped through the pages of a book.

I stopped in front of her and cleared my voice. "I'm looking for Donna."

The woman glanced at me and held up a finger. She grabbed a radio from the cradle next to her and whispered into it.

"Please wait right over there." The woman gestured to a bench along the left wall.

I nodded and backed away from the table. The space felt like the mix of a library and a museum. I got the impression that if I spoke in anything above a whisper, the woman behind the desk would glare daggers at me. I took a seat on the bench and tried not to fidget while I waited.

Five minutes later, a woman rushed into the room. She was petite, maybe an inch or two over five feet. She shoved a pen into her cardigan pocket and marched toward me. Her hands flew over her short, graying bob, straightening a few flyways as she crossed the room. She came to a stop a few feet away and shoved her hand out. "I'm Donna, Donna Shaw. And you are?"

I scrambled to my feet and shook her hand. "Dani Williams. Willow recommended I speak with you. I'm doing some research into an old resident."

Donna nodded. "If the resident was mentioned in the news at all, I'll have a record of them here. What era are you looking at?"

"The 1940s."

She turned on her heel and marched out of the room. I blinked and darted after her. I trailed behind her by a few feet as she walked through a doorway at the back of the room. The feeling of being in a library intensified as I followed her. We passed a series of study rooms before she took a sharp turn at the end of the hall into her own office.

Her desk was covered with files. They were neatly arranged into stacks, with sticky notes plastered across the top file in each stack. Her handwriting was blocky and precise. *Document Requests from the Seattle Times.* I took a seat across from her as she booted up her computer.

"What name are you looking for?" Donna asked.

"The first one is Booker Lancaster," I said.

She typed it in then leaned forward in her seat, her brow furrowing. "No hits."

"Try Beau Lancaster."

"There are two hits for that one." Donna grabbed her sticky note pad and quickly jotted down some letters and numbers. "And the second name?"

"Mac Turner."

She repeated the process, writing down a few more numbers.

"Any more?"

I shook my head.

She ripped the note from the pad, stood, and marched

back out of the room. I stared at her retreating back, wide-eyed. I surged to my feet and ran to keep up. She led me to one of the study rooms and asked me to wait. She didn't wait for a response before turning away to disappear up a flight of stairs.

I paced the room. A pressure was building at the back of my head. Whenever I was about to encounter something momentous, my powers of divination liked to point it out by giving me headaches. It was useful although not entirely pleasant. I took the building pressure as a good sign that I was in the right place.

After a few minutes of waiting, Donna returned with a box. She deposited it gently next to a blocky contraption that I recognized from my college days: a microfiche reader. It was like an old-school TV connected to a microscope. In a way, it reminded me of some of the equipment I had in my darkroom at home.

"Have you used one of these before?" she asked.

I nodded.

She stepped back into the doorway and pointed at a cart. "Put the slides back there when you are done. And if you need anything further, ask for me at the front desk."

I opened my mouth to thank her, but she was gone again. Chuckling, I put my bag down and sat in front of the microfiche reader. Perched on the stool, I slid the first of the cards into the machine and located the article Donna had jotted down for me. It was a front-page story about WWII vets coming home at the end of the war. It had a photo of a group of men standing in uniform in front of a boat. Beau stood off to the side, the only member of his unit present. He was easy to spot because he was the only Black man in the photo. His name was in the caption under the picture, but I couldn't find any mention of him in the article itself.

I stared at him. While everyone else in the photo was relaxed and smiling, he stood straight and stiff, his hands behind his back. He had his cap on, shielding his eyes from the light. I reread the article. All the other units were mentioned but his. I furrowed my brow and leaned closer to the machine. He wore a silver star. Only one other soldier in the photo had a silver star, and two paragraphs were dedicated to his gallantry.

Shaking my head, I removed the microfiche and grabbed the next card. I slid it into place. The next mention of Beau Lancaster was the classified ad his sister had put out. It had a small photo of him. In that one, he was smiling. His hair was neatly trimmed, and he had a sparkle in his eyes. Something about his gentle smile was mischievous. It warmed up his face and made me instantly like him. I read through the ad.

> MISSING PERSON – PLEASE HELP
>
> I am searching for my beloved brother, Beau Lancaster, a brave World War II veteran and cherished member of our family. Beau was last seen in Point Pleasant, Washington, on November 14th, 1945. He stands around 5'11", with a strong build, warm brown eyes, and a kind smile that could light up any room. He was wearing black pants and a white shirt.
>
> Beau served his country with honor and returned home to seek peace and happiness. If you saw him or know anything about his whereabouts, I am begging for your help. Even the smallest piece of information could mean the world to our family.
>
> Contact: Ida Lancaster, 1547 Charles Ave.

Beau had been home just over two months when he disappeared. I chewed on my lip as I reread it, taking in all the details. It didn't tell me much. *Why did they place only one ad?* Imani mentioned that they'd lost their home soon after. Maybe one ad was all they could afford.

I put his slide away and looked at the short list for Mac Turner. His first slide was the same one I'd pulled out for

Beau. He had been included in the lineup in the photos. They returned from war the same day. The second mention of him was from a few years later, in 1947. He was opening a veterans hall in Point Pleasant.

The hairs on my neck stood on end, and the pressure at the back of my head spiked as the door behind me opened. I glanced over my shoulder, and my mouth went dry as Delaney glided into the room. She held my gaze with her mismatched-color eyes before stepping to the side to let her companion enter after her. *Two Wardens.* My heart raced, and I fought the urge to bolt.

Delaney's companion was not as unusual looking as Delaney, although she was still very striking. She had angular features that seemed even sharper with her piercing blue eyes. Her black hair was pulled back into a neat French braid. She wore a floor-length dress that billowed around her legs as she walked. I turned back toward the machine.

I didn't have anything else to read, but I stared at the screen anyway. *What do I do?* Chairs scraped against the floorboards. I peeked behind me as they took seats, their eyes focused on my back. The alarm bell went off in my head as one of them attempted to read my mind. It was like fingers poking inside my head. I swayed in my seat and focused on maintaining the mental shield as their magic clawed at it. Delaney's darkness wrapped around my ankles, holding me in place.

I gritted my teeth and panned the screen forward to the next image and continued reading. The words swam in front of me. I had a hard time focusing on the screen. It took everything I had to keep the shields. I didn't have the strength to stand, not with Delaney holding me there. I leaned forward onto the machine and carefully read the articles. If they were going to slip through my defenses, then all I wanted them to get was the words from these useless articles.

Slowly, I read one article after another. They ranged in topic from a story about a recent storm blowing a fishing vessel off course to a sinkhole at a logging operation to the unveiling of a war memorial. I scrolled through them one by one, willing my legs to move. Sweat rolled down my back as I strained to keep my secrets hidden.

When I was skimming over an article about more property downtown being purchased by a guy named Harold, the alarm bells in my head stopped ringing. Delaney sighed.

I glanced behind myself. A flash of annoyance crossed her face before she could school her features. She shook her head. *Good. Be frustrated.* I hunched my shoulders and held my breath as they stood. Their heels clicked against the wooden floors as they left.

Then the door opened and closed. The hairs on the back of my neck went down. The pressure at the back of my head subsided. I exhaled and slumped on the stool. I glanced down at my phone, and my eyes widened. Four hours had passed. The experience of me willfully sitting there, keeping them out of my head, had all blurred together. But it hadn't felt like four hours. I rechecked the protection spell. It was still in place.

I had outlasted them.

They had left without getting anything useful from me.

My legs shook when I finally stood, collected my bag, and left. The human body wasn't meant to sit on an uncomfortable wooden stool for so long. Everything ached. The image of Chris's oversize jet bathtub flitted through my mind. Relaxing into that would have to wait. I had to warn the others that at least two Wardens were in town. Unlike Delaney's first visit, I hadn't promised not to tell my coven mates about this one.

CHAPTER 9

The sun was setting as I parked outside the Bizzy Bean. I walked inside and caught Heather's eye. I cocked my head to the side, jerking it toward the back booth. She nodded and smiled at the next customer in line. I pushed my way through the plexiglass doors into the cat enclosure and stalked past a group of kittens playing in the center of the room. I claimed my usual seat and sat, shoulders hunched, waiting for Heather. While I waited, I pulled out my phone and texted the group chat.

> **DANI:**
> I've got an update. Meet me at the Bizzy Bean ASAP.

Within seconds, Megan and the Retirees read the message. Megan sent a thumbs-up emoji. I tucked my phone into my pocket and tried not to stew on things. Watching the kittens as they darted back and forth across the room, scampering after a battery-powered feathered mouse, would normally bring a smile to my face. Something about being surrounded by playful cats was calming. But even their cute antics weren't enough to fully relieve the stress of the day. By the time Heather slid into the booth across from me, the strain had only partially lifted from my shoulders.

"Everything all right?" Heather asked.

I shook my head. "I've got an update. The others should be on their way soon."

Heather nodded. "I'll ask Becca to take over the counter for a while, then."

She slid out from the booth without another word and returned to the counter. She whispered to Becca. I sank into the booth, my gaze sliding around the room. It was half filled with regulars. As Heather made her way back to the booth, Megan arrived.

On her way through the room, Megan stopped only momentarily to scoop up a cat, one of the older kittens, a pure-white one with blue eyes that were slightly crossed. She plopped down in the seat opposite me and stroked the cat as it found a comfortable place to sit on her lap. "Busy day?" she asked.

"Ish? A lot happened."

She nodded, and we sat in silence until the Retirees arrived a few minutes later. They shuffled into the room as one unit and made their way to our table. Agnes claimed the seat next to me, while Betty took the seat next to Megan. Sarah grabbed two chairs from a nearby table and stood, fidgeting with her puffy jacket's zipper.

"The Wardens are in town," I said.

The table froze. The news wasn't unexpected, but it still made everyone at the table tense. Agnes pulled out a salt-shaker from her purse. My eyebrow rose as she poured salt into her palm. It was a spell I'd seen her cast before. It helped prevent eavesdropping. The table sat in silence as she murmured over her palm, the iridescent shimmers of her magic settling over the salt. She scattered it around us, enveloping the table in a glittering globe.

"What happened?" Betty asked.

Megan leaned forward in her seat, her hand reaching across the table toward me. "Did you speak to them?"

"Not exactly." I sighed. "They showed up at the historical society while I was there. That spell that protects against mind reading works. I could hear the mental alarm as it went off. They did not look happy about that."

"They?" Sarah inched forward in her seat. "How many are there?"

"Two." I gritted my teeth. No matter how much I wanted to tell them about Delaney's midnight visit, the words wouldn't come out. I sighed and instead quickly explained what I could about my day, from my talk to Imani to what I'd found out at the historical society.

"Just to make sure I'm understanding this correctly"—Heather held up her hand—"Meredith Walker and Beau Lancaster were in a relationship, which upset a lot of people at the time. Beau went missing... and just a few months later, Meredith cursed her entire coven?"

I nodded. "I know in my gut they're connected. I just don't know how yet."

"Do you think..." Heather glanced around the table and swallowed. "Do you think your great grandmother's coven might have had something to do with his death?"

Agnes shifted uncomfortably next to me. Sarah looked like she had eaten something sour. I glanced toward Betty, who snorted and crossed her arms over her chest.

"No way," Betty said. "It's not something our moms would have done."

Megan placed her hand on Betty's shoulder. "We never like to think poorly of our loved ones—"

Betty shrugged her hand off. "It's not that we don't want to think poorly of them. My mom wasn't perfect. But she was no killer. She was a good person. She wouldn't have done something to hurt Beau."

"Are you sure?" Heather asked.

"Positive," Sarah said.

I held up my hands. "All right. Maybe they weren't involved. But there is still a connection there. Can we all agree on that?"

Betty turned her head and looked away.

Agnes leaned forward in her seat, her hand reaching toward her partner. "Betty?"

Betty sighed and pinched the bridge of her nose. "Fine. I can admit there's a connection. Just... don't paint my mom as a villain."

"Okay," I said.

The tension hanging over the table eased as Betty relaxed into her seat.

"Do you know anything about Beau Lancaster? I know you didn't recognize the name Booker, but does 'Beau' ring any bells?" I asked.

Sarah pursed her lips. "Actually, I think it does."

"The ghost story?" Agnes asked.

Sarah nodded.

I straightened in my seat. "What ghost story?"

"Johnny Foster used to babysit us when we were kids," Sarah said.

"I don't remember the details anymore," Agnes added.

Betty dropped her hands to her lap. "But I remember him saying the name Beau during one of the ghost stories he used to tell us before bed. They weren't all exactly ghost stories. But that's what he liked to call them. He liked to scare us."

Sarah nodded. "Don't go outside, or you'll end up like Beau. I remember that."

"Johnny Foster? The original owner of the Crab Shack?" I asked.

The Retirees nodded in unison.

I chewed on my lip. I had two leads: Mac Turner and a ghost story told by Johnny Foster. It was better than nothing.

"All right, the update is done. You ladies mind if I call Kim for a minute? I want to make sure Grace is okay." I gestured to the bubble around us that prevented eavesdropping. I wouldn't be able to call Kim once the spell dropped.

Agnes nodded.

I pulled out my phone and dialed.

Kim picked up on the fourth ring. In the background were sounds of kids playing. "What?"

I spluttered. "How's Grace?"

Kim sighed. A message popped up on my screen asking if I agreed to a Facetime. I clicked Yes. The phone was angled up sharply toward Kim's face, like she was holding it at her waist. She didn't say a word. The photos on the walls bobbed up and down as she made her way through her house.

"Kim?" I asked.

She opened a door and rotated the camera. Grace lay in the same position as I'd last seen her. She was still, her dark-brown hair fanned out around her head. I bit my knuckle, my eyes tearing up as I stared at her. She looked so small on the bed.

"She's the quietest house guest I've ever had. I reapplied the sleeping spell twenty minutes ago and moved her a little so she wouldn't get any bedsores."

"Thank you," I croaked.

The camera flipped back around to Kim's face. She glowered at me, her blue eyes fierce. "Like I had a choice."

"Still..." I wiped a tear from my eyes and cleared my throat. "Thank you."

She snorted. "I'm counting down the days until she's not my problem."

I said goodbye and disconnected the call then shoved my phone into my pocket. She had only promised to watch Grace for a week. I had to figure out how to save Grace sooner rather than later, or I would lose her to the Wardens.

Sarah peered at me, her head cocked to the side. "We still have a few boxes of my mom's stuff we can go through. We'll tackle that. There might be something in there that could help."

"I'll track down Johnny and Mac and see what they remember," I said.

Megan nodded. "And I'll keep an eye on the tendrils, to make sure they don't spread to any other new locations."

Heather glanced around the table. "And I'll... keep the coffee pot on?"

Betty patted her shoulder. "Don't discount your contributions, hon. You have no idea how helpful it is to have a place we can all come and feel at ease. You do a lot to keep this group sane."

Heather brightened. "Sanity guardian, reporting for duty."

I cleared my throat. "We all have our assignments, then."

"Yeah." Megan sighed.

The whole table was silent for a moment. The situation almost felt surreal. Outside those walls, we didn't feel safe. But there, we were secure. There, we had hope. And we had Heather to thank for that. The moment we stood to go tackle our to-do lists, the peaceful moment would be gone.

Betty was the first to stand. The other Retirees quickly followed suit. We all filtered out of the booth and one by one patted the white cat in Megan's lap for luck before walking toward the exit.

I walked in a daze to my car. It was too late in the day to track down my two targets. Johnny had retired well over a decade before. While he was still a regular at the Crab Shack, he was usually only there on the weekends. I would have to wait until the next day to try to track him down. I drove back to Chris's place, dreaming of his jacuzzi bathtub as I made my way through town.

Chris was working late. His car wasn't in the driveway when I pulled up in front of his townhome. I parked as far to the right as I could. His driveway was narrow, and his garage barely counted as a two-car garage. I parked out front and walked up to the front door, my day playing through my mind. I froze as my hand settled on the doorknob.

My jaw clenched, and my neck stiffened. Pressure formed between my eyes as my nose wrinkled. Annoyance radiated off the door. I replayed the morning in my head. I hadn't touched the front door, but Chris had when he left. But the emotional residue didn't feel like his. The emotions someone left behind on an object were unique to a person. Everyone's annoyance felt different. I knew what Chris felt like, and that wasn't it. Someone else had touched the door.

I swallowed and unlocked it, pushing the door inward. I was greeted by silence. My heart skipped a beat as I stepped inside. The hairs on the back of my neck rose. On instinct, I reached out and touched the light switch. The same annoyance I'd felt on the doorknob was there. Whoever had touched the door had been inside the house. My mouth went dry. I scanned the room. Nothing was out of place, at least as far as I could tell. The remote was still on the arm of the couch. The cushions were in the same place I'd left them after cuddling with Chris before we headed out for the day. My gaze slid across the photos on the walls. Chris had an old photo of him and his dad next to the hallway that led to the kitchen.

I crossed to it, my fingers hovering over his face, and smiled. "Let's see who was here."

I mumbled the words to the spell that would let me see into the past. I could access the senses of an object. To see the past, the object had to have eyes to do so, either eyes in a photo or eyes of a camera. Golden motes flowed straight from my mouth to the photo. The stronger I got, the less the motes darted around. Instead, they went in an almost straight line from my mouth to the eyes in the photograph. I touched the photo and fought back a gasp as the room brightened and the past played for me behind my eyelids.

The sun was sinking outside at about the time I would

have arrived at the Bizzy Bean. The front door opened, and Delaney and the other Warden stepped inside. They walked straight through the room and past the photo. They disappeared for about ten minutes before reappearing. Delaney stalked out of the room, almost slamming the door shut behind herself. The other one stood in the middle of the room for a minute, unmoving, with her back to the hallway. She eventually turned and stared straight at the photo on the wall. She pursed her lips and followed her associate, turning the light off behind herself. The annoyance had been the mystery Warden's. *What was she annoyed about? Did she know I would be watching her later?*

My eyes flew open as another thought hit me. Charlie hadn't greeted me at the door.

I stumbled back from the wall, my heart beating a mile a minute. My whole body shook. I held my hands to my chest, trying to still myself. I hadn't felt any alarms from him throughout the day. If he was in trouble, I would have felt it. *Right?* I closed my eyes, sending out my thoughts to him. I felt him nearby. He was alone and scared. *Why didn't I feel that before?*

I charged through the house, following the connection to him. He was somewhere above me. I took the steps two at a time, pausing on the first landing then following the feeling upward to the top floor. I felt a tug at my heart, leading me forward to the bedroom. The door was closed. And the annoyance I'd felt downstairs lingered on the handle. I swallowed and pushed the door open. The lights were out, but I was close enough to Charlie to access his senses. The bed lay in the center of the room. It was perfectly made, with crisp corners. Chris was the type of guy who made his bed every morning. I stepped into the room, my senses questing outward. Charlie was so close, but I didn't see him in the room. I kneeled down and peered under the bed. It was empty.

Shaking my head, I stood and turned slowly in place. *What did they want in here?* I stopped, facing the closet. The gentle tug at my heart pulled me forward toward the closet doors. I slid it open, and Charlie launched himself at me. He flung his body, full force, against my chest, his paws wrapping around my neck. I stumbled back. He was a big boy, approaching fifteen pounds at only six months old. I cradled him in my arms as he meowed into my ear.

"I'm so sorry, buddy. Are you okay?"

He burrowed his head into my hair. After a few seconds, he settled down and purred into my ear. I sat down on the bed and petted him until he fell asleep.

What did they want in here? It felt like a violation. They'd broken into Chris's home while we were out and had been in his bedroom, where we slept. I chewed on my lip. I unfocused my eyes and searched the space for lingering spells. Nothing. *Did they find what they were looking for, or will they be back?*

I stroked Charlie's head while he slept. "I won't leave you alone again. Not while they're in town. I promise."

CHAPTER 10

The next morning, I put Charlie's harness on him and took him with me when I left Chris's townhome for the day. He sat quietly in the front seat and stared out the window as I drove through town toward the veterans hall. It was a squat single-story building not too far from the pier. The brick walls were painted white, with a black silhouette of soldiers raising a flag spray-painted near the front door. I parked in an open spot near the building and opened my car door. Charlie hopped across my lap and darted ahead of me to the sidewalk, where he stood waiting for me to catch up. I hooked his leash onto his harness and walked toward the entrance.

The inside of the building had a different feel from the exterior. It had warmer tones, with a cherry wood floor and leather-bound mahogany chairs. A large display case filled with photos took up a large section of the foyer wall.

A younger gentleman with a blond buzz cut stood as I entered. He strode toward me, his gait uneven. "Can I help you, ma'am?"

"I'm looking for someone. I hope he still frequents the hall. His name's Mac Turner."

He nodded, his eyes flicking to Charlie at my feet. "You're in luck. He's here most days. He just arrived."

I glanced down at Charlie. "He's a good kitty. Better on a leash than most dogs."

The guy chuckled and ran his hand across his head. "I was just thinking that, ma'am. I've never seen a cat being walked before."

"Where can I find Mac?" I asked.

He straightened and pointed toward the hallway. "Straight back. He'll be reading in the last room at the end of the hall. You'll probably find him near the pool tables. Although he doesn't play much these days."

I thanked him and followed his directions down the hall. The walls were covered in photos of soldiers with small plaques underneath. The photos shifted through the decades, starting in black-and-white at the beginning of the hall and transitioning to color farther down. The uniforms morphed through the ages, from the classic look of the 1940s, to the deep greens of the Vietnam era, to the browns and desert grays of the more recent uniforms. Voices were at the end of the hall, muffled conversations punctuated by joy-filled laughter.

I poked my head through the door at the end of the hallway. It opened into a large recreational room. Along one wall were more cabinets filled with photos. A large TV covered one wall, with big, overstuffed chairs lined up in front of it. Behind the chairs and taking up most of the room was a series of pool and foosball tables, with some round poker tables at the back. Sitting beyond the tables, nestled in an armchair by big bay windows, was Mac Turner.

He was wrapped in a sweater. His hair was completely gray. He peered down at a book in his hands through bifocal lenses. He licked his finger to turn a page. I studied him for a few seconds before entering the room. He looked small in his chair, and his thin hands were spotted. He glanced at me as I approached, his blue eyes watery. "Is that a cat?" His voice didn't have any of his physical frailty. It was older but firm. He had a deep voice with a commanding edge. I got the impression he was someone who was used to having people under him pay attention.

I put on a professional smile. "It is. His name is Charlie. Are you Mac Turner?"

Mac folded his book into his lap. "I am. Most people call me Marcus these days. Mac was a name for a younger man."

"Mind if I sit?" I gestured to a seat across from him.

"By all means." He watched me as I sat down. "Now, Miss...?"

"Williams," I offered.

"Miss Williams, what can this old man do for you today? You aren't with another one of those papers, are you? I've given enough interviews over the founding of this place. I know, I know, you all want one last word before I hit a hundred and croak."

Something about being in his presence seemed easy. He felt comforting, like I was talking to my grandfather. I shook my head and reminded myself that he wasn't George. "No. I'm investigating the body that was recently found at the sheriff's station. I understand you served together."

He blinked. "Body? What body?"

"Beau Lancaster."

He froze, and something shifted behind his eyes. He stared at me, speechless. I leaned toward him, brushing my fingers against his seat. My skin tingled as a coldness seeped into my core. My heart became heavy in my chest as grief and shock warred with each other.

"He was found earlier this week," I said.

Marcus pushed himself to his feet. He took a faltering step forward and braced himself against the windowsill. "I haven't heard that name in decades."

"I take it that means you remember him."

He nodded. "We didn't serve directly together. Not in the same unit, anyway. They were all segregated back then."

That's a lot of grief for someone who didn't serve directly with him. Maybe they got close after? I moved to stand next to him, leaning my arm against the windowsill. The same grief from the chair lingered on the wood. I softened my voice. "I thought you might have known each other better than that."

"I knew Beau as well as anyone could." He closed his eyes. "I owe him my life."

"Can you tell me about him?"

"The first time we met was on the beach. It was an island in the Pacific. We were under fire. Half my unit was scrambling backward, trying to get to the boat. His unit was racing forward. A bullet hit me in the thigh, and I went down. I really thought I was going to die right there. But these massive hands grabbed me and yanked me up. He threw me over his shoulder like I weighed nothing and hightailed it up the embankment. And what did he get in thanks? Puke down his back."

My throat thickened as he shifted from grief to nostalgia.

"He carried me for over a mile until he found a safe cave for us to hole up in. He and I and six other guys stayed there for three days, waiting for reinforcements to arrive. Lucky for me, he had some basic medical knowledge, so I didn't bleed to death."

"I heard that things were tense when you all got back from the war."

Marcus sighed. "I came back as a war hero. And he came back still a Black man. His service record didn't mean much to most people."

"I heard it had something to do with a woman? A woman named Meredith?" I held my breath. For a millisecond, I felt the mood shifting, but he stepped away from the window, and I lost it.

"He was a reckless fool." He put his hands behind his

back. "In war, being brave is admirable. But here? Here, it just got him in trouble. I should have been a better friend."

He stopped and stared out the window. I watched him and held on to the silence. I could sense there was more to it, and I had to be patient.

"I told him he was being an idiot and not to call if he got into trouble." His voice broke on the word *not*. The rest of the sentence came out wet with unshed tears. "What if I hadn't said that? Would things be different?" He turned away and faced the wall. He cleared his throat, wiping at his face.

"Who did you think Beau was going to get into trouble with?" I asked.

Marcus shrugged. "It was tense back then. A different time. The whole town had opinions on his relationship with Meredith."

"Was there anyone in particular who was upset?" I pressed.

He looked at me over his shoulder. His gaze hardened. "A few. I know he really got into it with his business partner. It's what we fought about. He wanted me to talk sense into Frankie, but Frankie and I agreed he was asking for trouble, dating that woman."

"Frankie?" I only knew one Frankie who could fit the bill. I was praying he wouldn't say the name.

"Frankie Gardner."

My heart sank at the words.

"He used to run a bakery around here."

Frankie Gardner used to make my favorite dessert, the same one Chris had recreated when he told me he wanted to be a couple. That complicated things. *Hey, honey, mind setting up a meeting so I can interrogate your childhood mentor?* Chris and Frankie were still in contact, so he would be the best person to set up a meeting. I was sure that conversation was going to go swimmingly. I forced a smile onto my face and thanked Marcus for his time.

Marcus Turner was off my suspect list. His grief had been palpable. He wasn't hiding anything, as far as I could tell. And Frankie, the lovable baker from my youth, was now on it.

Charlie scampered ahead of me to my car. I sank into the front seat and closed my eyes. I couldn't wrap my head around the idea that Frankie was a violent man. My memories of him involved him singing, his voice a smooth baritone as he belted out show tunes while he tossed donuts from the hot oil onto the cooling rack. Whenever I came up to my gran's from California, I would invariably end up seated at his counter with my friends, watching him work. He mostly made baked goods, but he also had an old soda fountain, which made his place feel like a diner straight out of a fifties film. I struggled to label him as a suspect, but that was purely an emotional response. I didn't know Frankie that well. One thing I had learned over the years was that someone's outward facade was rarely a clear indication of who they were inside.

Sighing, I pulled out my phone. I had to treat the lead like any other. And the first place I always started was with a person's online profiles. I scrunched my nose as I scrolled through his page. He was spotty at best at updating it. He hadn't posted anything in well over a year, and his posts before that were sporadic. He would post things a few days in a row then nothing for a month. It seemed to ebb and flow based on when he was spending time with his great grandkids. He posted more when they were with him, usually about the adventures they got up to. The last post was about the youngest going off to college. He probably didn't see them much anymore. That explained the absence. My heart clenched. He was a family man. Poking around like that felt wrong.

I swallowed the discomfort and did a wider search for him online. I found a single news article about the closure of his famous donut shop. I scrolled through the story and paused. *After seven failed attempts to open, Frankie's finally found its home on Washington Avenue.*

Seven failed attempts? That's a lot. He'd been on Washington my entire life. I hadn't realized he had struggled to open the joint. I pursed my lips and exhaled slowly as I typed out a message to Imani.

> **DANI:**
> This is Dani Williams. We spoke the other day about your uncle. I was wondering if the name Frankie Gardner means anything to you.

I dropped my phone into my lap and stared out the window, contemplating my next move. Charlie stared at me from the passenger seat. He stepped onto my lap and head-butted my shoulder.

"I'm just thinking, buddy." I scratched his head.

My phone dinged as a new message came in.

> **IMANI:**
> My mom worked for him for a few years, but he had to let her go after some vandalism incidents.

I furrowed my brow.

> **DANI:**
> Vandalism incidents?

> **IMANI:**
> Yeah. My mom at the end kept trying to get ready for her job there. Some days she remembered that he had let her go. Others, she didn't. Some days she would talk about how he kept paying her for a few weeks after he laid her off, and without him she wouldn't have made it.

DANI:
That was nice of him.

IMANI:
While it didn't help her keep the house, it helped her afford the bus ticket cross country. When my mom talked about it, it felt like he was trying to make up for something. She denied it though and said he was just being a good friend.

DANI:
Did Frankie and Beau ever have a falling out?

IMANI:
Not that I know of. But maybe? From what my mom said, the whole town was against Beau.

DANI:
Did other people do things?

IMANI:
Small things. No one wanted to answer her questions or help. Even the paper didn't want to take her money for better ad placement. My mom was still mad about that until the day she died. She was convinced that if she got into the Sunday paper, she would have finally found someone who saw something. But I guess we will never know.

That explained why she only placed one ad. *I wonder if the vandalism incident made the paper.* I wasn't ready to broach the subject of interviewing Frankie with Chris yet, so I opted for more research first. I punched in the address for the historical society into my GPS and drove.

The street outside the historical archive was crowded when I arrived. Yellow cones blocked access to the street, with a large sign overhead declaring it a farmers' market.

Despite the cold weather, a cluster of stalls had been erected to sell produce and wares from local artists and artisans. I found a spot to park three blocks away and walked over. Charlie sniffed the air as we passed a food stall selling Nutella-filled crepes. My stomach rumbled as the scent hit me. I couldn't risk the Wardens cornering me on an empty stomach, so I made a quick stop to pick one up. The nice vendor added slices of banana for no extra charge, then Charlie and I were off again.

I licked the last of the Nutella off my fingers as we strode into the historical society. The door closed behind me, cutting off the sounds of the street. Silence enveloped me as I crossed the room. The same woman from the day before sat behind the counter. She glanced up at me. "Here for Donna again?"

I nodded. "And the restroom. I need to wash my hands."

She grabbed the phone and spoke into it, her hand half covering the mouthpiece. When she was done, she set it back down and gave me a cool, professional smile. "She'll be right down." She grabbed a bottle of hand sanitizer from a drawer and pushed it toward me. "For your hands."

The sanitizer was cold. Charlie hated the smell. His strong distaste flowed through our bond. I tried to breathe through my mouth to avoid the overpowering hospital scent as I rubbed my hands together. I backed away from the desk and took a seat in the waiting area.

When my bottom just touched the seat, Donna strode into the room. She marched up to me and thrust her hand out. "More research?" she asked.

I scrambled to my feet and shook her hand. "Yep. I'm now looking for any records you might have regarding Frankie Gardner."

Donna turned away from me without a word and walked down the hallway. She walked fast for such a short woman. I darted after her and power walked to keep up. Willow had described her as sweet, but she struck me as coldly efficient. But maybe she was different once you got to know her.

She didn't sit when she arrived at her office. She leaned over her keyboard and typed in Frankie's name before grabbing a Post-it note and scribbling a few numbers and letters across it. Without a word, she was on the move again. She left me waiting in the same reading room while she fetched the records. She came back with a few different boxes. She stuck the sticky note on the top box and handed it to me. "Put them back on the cart when you're done."

I nodded, and she was gone.

I exhaled and took a seat on the stool. My muscles objected. My back didn't appreciate being in that position again, hunched over the microfiche reader. Charlie rubbed his head against my legs then lay down out of the way while I worked.

Most of the articles were from between 1946 and 1951. They ranged from small mentions of his first location closing its doors due to a string of vandalism events to a kitchen fire at his second, a mysterious rat infestation at his third, and even more vandalism at his fourth, fifth, and sixth locations. Finally, in 1951, he found his location on Washington Street, and the series of vandalism abruptly ended. I pursed my lips and read through other crime blotters for the same period. The reporting was sparse. Some weeks included a crime section. Other weeks were bare. In one article, crime was down, and a month later, crime was at an all-time high. I found no rhyme or reason to how it was reported. I couldn't tell if the incidents involving Frankie's were par for the course for the time or if he really was cursed. Or being harassed. I leaned back and stared at the timeline I'd put together on a piece of scratch paper.

I sighed and pinched the bridge of my nose.

Donna's voice broke into my thoughts. "Did you find what you were looking for?"

I jumped at the sound. I spun in my seat and stared at her hovering in the doorway. "I didn't hear you come in."

Donna stepped farther into the room. "I was passing by and noticed you sitting deep in thought."

I glanced back down at my timeline and hastily written notes. It was a mess. "Maybe?"

"Is there someone else you need me to look up?"

I shook my head. "I'm just having a hard time making sense of things. The reporting seems a bit sporadic."

"The newspaper was new back then. It was... spotty at best for the first few years."

"Great." I hung my head. "Just what I needed."

"You know," Donna said, taking another step into the room, "if you want to know something about the early days of the Island County Gazette, about stories that didn't make the cut, you need to talk to Benjamin Hayes. He was the original editor-in-chief."

I sat up and smiled.

"He's still around and does the occasional function. I have the number for his assistant in my office. I can get it for you."

"That would be fantastic."

Without another word, she turned on her heel and marched out of the room. I tidied up the pile of slides and put them back on the cart while I waited. After a couple of minutes, she returned with another sticky note and handed it to me. As I took it from her, warmth spread through my body. The emotions on the paper were joyful at a job well done. Her face was placid, not revealing her happier thoughts. "Here you go."

"Thanks, Donna."

I followed her out. She turned and waved as I headed toward the front door. Willow was right. Donna was kind, just a little awkward about it.

Charlie and I walked back past the farmers' market as we headed toward the car. It was winding down, and a few of the stalls were closing shop for the evening. On my way to the car, I grabbed two savory crepes filled with chicken, mushrooms, and melted gruyere cheese along with a heaping side of harvest salad. I texted Chris to let him know I had dinner then called Benjamin's assistant. I left a voice mail requesting a meeting then drove home to Chris's place.

CHAPTER 11

I had a hard time falling asleep. My thoughts kept wandering to the Wardens and my daughter lying unconscious in a stranger's house. I rechecked the doors and windows five times before I could convince myself to stay in bed. I wore myself out, recasting all the protection spells I knew. But even with that, if not for Chris holding me and whispering into my ear that everything was going to be okay, I probably wouldn't have fallen asleep until dawn. As it was, I was still awake well past midnight.

I silently thanked him as I collapsed into the chair opposite Olivia at the Pleasant View Insurance Agency. It was almost lunchtime, but I was still dragging because of the late night.

Charlie stalked around the office, looking under every desk and peering into the break room. He glanced at me, cocking his head to one side in question. While our bond didn't allow for direct communication, I could still sense his emotions and had gotten good at guessing his thoughts. Today he was thinking, *Where's Bailey?*

I chuckled and patted my leg. "She isn't here today, buddy."

He trotted past Olivia, his nose held in the air, and claimed my lap.

Olivia laughed. "Sorry, little fella. Zac has her today. They're going to the dog park."

"I'm sure he will forgive you. Eventually." I scratched behind Charlie's ears.

"Thank goodness." Olivia smiled. "How are things going at the station?"

"It's largely on hold right now, pending the sheriff's office releasing the scene. I heard through the grapevine that the forensics guys are finishing up today, so in theory, we should be back in business by this time tomorrow. Once the demo crew can get back in there, it should be only a few more days before we have a clear image of what needs to happen. I was planning to follow behind them and sketch out some ideas floor by floor then to run those ideas past the committee before requesting quotes."

"Excellent." Olivia clapped. "Thank you again for helping out with this."

"I'm happy to"—my phone rang in my pocket, and I fumbled for it—"help."

"Miss Williams?" the voice was unfamiliar. It had a slight accent and sounded androgynous. I couldn't place where the person was from.

"This is she."

"Are you still interested in a meeting with Mr. Hayes?" the person asked.

"Yes, of course I am. When would he be available?"

"He has an unexpected opening in his schedule. If you can be by his home in the next thirty minutes, we can squeeze you in. If not, then he does have some availability next week."

"Now's good." I grabbed a notebook from my purse. "What's his address?"

The assistant rattled it off and disconnected the call after confirming again that I could be there in time.

I shoved my phone into my bag and grabbed Charlie's leash. "I've got to go."

"So soon?" Olivia asked.

"I have an interview thing."

Olivia raised her eyebrow. "All right. I get it. A murder victim has been found. Who are you questioning now?"

I quickly filled her in on my investigation, in very broad strokes, as I got Charlie back into his harness.

"Good luck," she said as I scurried out the door.

Benjamin Hayes's home wasn't far from the office. He lived only a few blocks from the downtown area, in one of the oldest parts of Point Pleasant. In that section of town, the homes were spread far apart, with only one or two of them on a given block. The homes themselves were not sprawling estates, but they had an elegance to them: old wood and wrought-iron finishings. I parked in the driveway, made room in my oversize purse for Charlie, and got out. Charlie curled up in my bag and purred reassuringly as I made my way up the drive. My shoulder ached already from carrying him. The extra fifteen pounds was going to be a strain.

I huffed as I turned onto the walkway. The lawn was still green, and seasonal flowers were blooming. Everything about the home screamed old money. I knocked on the front door. My skin crawled as the feeling of being watched settled over me. I glanced up at a small camera over the door and smiled. A few seconds later, the front door opened, revealing a slender man dressed in a black suit. He was a few inches taller than me, with short but stylish blond hair. "Miss Williams?" he asked. The accent was even stronger in person. I still couldn't place it.

"That's me." I smiled and thrust my hand out.

He shook it and guided me through the home to a study in the back. The interior of the home was as finely crafted as the exterior. Small details were everywhere, indicating that most of the furniture had been hand built. The study was an impressive room. A large wooden desk took up the center of the room, with built-in bookshelves flanking it. The walls were covered with awards and photos of the same smiling man shaking hands with every mayor or person of interest the town had ever had. I swallowed as I came to a stop in front of the table.

Benjamin Hayes stared up at me through wire-rimmed spectacles that rested on his hawkish nose. Gray, wispy hair covered only half of his balding head. He was dressed warmly, in a well-pressed black shirt and a plush smoking jacket over it. He held his hand out, his fingers trembling, and gestured to the seat across from him. "Miss Williams. A pleasure to meet you. Can Gregory get you anything to drink?"

"A water would be fantastic." I took the offered chair.

"Your message said it was an urgent matter."

"Yes." I pulled a notepad out of my purse. "Somewhat. I had some questions for you about the early days of the paper."

"I suppose once a question has popped into the mind, it always feels urgent, especially to the young. Please, proceed."

I cleared my throat. "I was looking through articles from the late 1940s, and it seemed... inconsistent on whether or not there was a crime spree going on."

Benjamin laughed. He dabbed at his eyes as Gregory swept back into the room with a tray in hand. He set a hot cup of tea down in front of Benjamin and an iced water down next to me before ducking back out of the room. He was in and out so quickly that I barely had time to thank him.

"So... the crime spree?" I asked.

"I'm sorry for laughing. This town was so much sleepier than it is now. People got overly excited about small things. Honestly, it sold more papers when we sensationalized the petty crimes." He shoved his kerchief back into place.

"Although, to be frank, it didn't always sit right with me. I was young. I struggled with figuring out what was more important, accurate reporting or selling papers. When you had to sell papers to keep the doors open, though, sometimes the accurate reporting took a back seat. I'm proud to say, once we had the readership, that tendency went away. It just took a few years for us to go through the growing pains."

"Crime wasn't much of a problem?" I asked.

"Things were... quieter then."

"So, a business being hit by vandals multiple times would have been considered unusual?"

"Is this off the record?" He raised an eyebrow.

"Just hypothetically speaking, would it have been considered unusual?"

He pursed his lips. "Hypothetically speaking, while things didn't typically get violent, there might have been some residents who were particular about what businesses were allowed in their neighborhoods. Hypothetically speaking, these individuals may have been overly rambunctious about expressing those opinions. With rocks, paint, and the occasional threatening note or small fire."

"I didn't see anything about that in the paper," I said.

"Purely hypothetically speaking again, no one appreciates a mirror being held up when things could be considered unflattering. Stories like that wouldn't have sold papers, and we needed the money."

I chewed on the inside of my lip. *If they needed the money, why didn't they take Beau's sister's? Unless the paper was run by one of those particular residents.* "I see. Do you remember who handled the classified section?"

"It would have been my secretary."

"Hypothetically speaking, do you know why your secretary wouldn't have run an ad?"

"To my knowledge, we rarely turned an ad away—only some inappropriate things boys liked to post on occasion."

"How about a missing persons ad?" I asked.

He narrowed his eyes, the warmth leaving his face. "Sometimes, we had an awkward number of ads. We tried to keep them to an even spread, either two or four pages, depending on the day of the week. If an ad would have spilled over onto an extra page, it was declined. We always gave priority to new ones, so if the ad had already been run, it would have been the first to go. Are you referencing a particular incident?"

"Yes, I'm trying to help someone."

He nodded and grabbed a pen from the desk. "If you give me a name or date, I still have some of my old records. I can look into it for you."

"Thank you. It would have been for Beau, also known as Booker Lancaster, sometime in November of 1945." I studied his face as I said the name.

He faltered before writing it, a stiffness in his mouth that hadn't been there before. "I'll look into it." He jabbed the pen as he finished writing the five. "Who did you say you were helping?"

"His niece, Imani. His body was recently found."

He glanced at his watch. "Oh gosh. Look at the time. I almost forgot that I have a call coming up soon that I must prepare for. If there isn't anything else, I apologize, but I must cut this conversation short for the day."

I stood and stepped forward and lightly touched the table as I held out my hand. A ringing sounded in my ears, and a knot formed in my stomach. I swayed on my feet as my knees tried to give out from under me. He was stunned and afraid.

I tried to keep a professional smile on my face. "Thank you so much for your time."

His skin was dry and paper thin under my fingers. He limply shook my hand then turned away. Gregory cleared his throat behind me. I followed him out, lingering for only a few seconds longer to collect my things. I studied Benjamin out of the corner of my eye as I put my notepad away. Charlie shifted in my purse to make room for it. I hadn't picked up guilt or anger from the desk but fear mixed with something secretive. Mr. Hayes was hiding something, and it was beginning to feel like a conspiracy.

CHAPTER 12

I was agitated after my meeting with Benjamin Hayes. Something about him was slimy. He encapsulated all the bad things I'd ever heard about reporters. I very much doubted he cared about the truth, past or present. To calm my nerves, I took Charlie on a walk along the pier. We found a bench on the beach, and I let my mind wander as I took a seat. I was at the point in my investigation where every rock I turned over only revealed more questions. My conversation with Benjamin had been enlightening. Imani had said her mom had trouble getting help from the town for finding her brother, but part of me naively thought she must have been exaggerating. Realizing that Point Pleasant had a darker history was uncomfortable. That history hadn't been as welcoming to everyone. I scrunched up my nose. On the other hand, Steven Bishop winning the mayoral election had been considered notable around town. He was the first Black man to sit in the seat. I shifted on the bench, a sour expression on my face as I stared out at the water.

I tried to block out the bitter thoughts and focus on my next steps. I still had to talk to Johnny Foster, the Retirees' babysitter with an unusual ghost story featuring Beau; interview Frankie Gardner, the former business partner; and inspect the crime scene. I needed Chris's help for two of them. I sighed and settled onto the bench. Charlie hopped up next to me and curled up, half on my lap, and looked out at the water with me. Together, we sat *patiently* waiting, a book in my hand, until the time came to get up and meet Chris for dinner. A few minutes before five, I stood from my bench on the beach and made my way up to the pier.

The Crab Shack sat halfway down the pier, the wooden structure suspended over the water on concrete pilings. A colorful banner hung over the entryway, announcing the opening of the winter crabbing season. I had beaten Chris there, which wasn't a surprise. He typically got off at five and would probably be a few more minutes. I went in ahead of him and put my name in for a window seat.

"Is Johnny around today?" I asked Martha Foster. She was the wife of Henry Foster, who had taken over running the crab shack from his father.

"Out fishing." Martha grabbed two menus from the stack and walked ahead of me to the table. "He should be back in tomorrow."

"Could you ask him to call me when he gets back in?" I asked.

She glanced at me over her shoulder. "Sure. Can I tell him what it's about?"

"A ghost story."

She flashed me a smile. "He's got a lot of those he likes to tell. If you go asking for one, prepare yourself for listening to at least six."

I claimed a seat facing the setting sun. "I'll make sure to have a thermos of hot chocolate to share, then. Ghost stories are best over a warm beverage."

"He'll love that." She left me with the menus.

I didn't make it into the Crab Shack too often. They specialized in crab boils, which was more like an event than just a meal. Martha would cart large pots of steamed crab, shrimp, corn on the cob, sausage links, and hefty chunks of potato, all coated in layers of spice and butter, out to the table. It was something people ate with their hands more than utensils and frequently required bibs. It was messy but delicious. They had other options on the menu, but they weren't nearly as popular. Most people came here for the crab boil, with either the old bay seasoning mix or the Cajun one. I preferred the Cajun. It came with a generous portion of the best garlic butter I'd ever eaten.

Chris arrived a few minutes later, just as the sun disappeared over the water. He plopped down on his chair opposite me, his face haggard. "Hope you weren't waiting long. It was... a difficult day at work. I couldn't get away on time."

I squeezed his hand. "Not long at all. What's going on?"

Chris's shoulders rounded forward as he collapsed in on himself. He ran his free hand through his hair. "Bob is really worked up over this case. I've never seen him like this before."

"I'm sorry, my love."

"He keeps vacillating between yelling and almost crying. Being a sheriff is his whole identity. His dad was. His grandfather was. His great grandfather was. It's like this body being found is an attack on who he is. I've never seen him feel so... violated? It's almost like a body was found in his backyard."

Waves of concern rolled off Chris. While he had his problems with Bob, he still respected the man. I couldn't say the same. His stubbornness had stood in the way of justice more than once since I'd moved to town. But Chris didn't need my snarky opinions right then. A man he respected was hurting.

I settled for a sympathetic expression as I rubbed a thumb against the back of his hand. "It's going to be okay."

He squeezed my hand back.

"I guess I should keep my case updates for after dinner."

He peered up at me, warmth in his eyes. "Thank you. I just need to unwind for a while. But once we exit those doors, you can give me all the updates."

"Deal." I leaned across the table to kiss him.

As I sat back down, Martha stopped by the table. "You guys ready to order?"

I glanced at Chris, who nodded. "Yeah. I'll take the Cajun crab boil. With extra butter."

Chris handed her his menu. "I'll take the same. And a sweet tea to drink."

She gathered the menus and strode away from the table, barking out the order as she reached the kitchen. I leaned on the table, my chin resting in my palms. "Other than the Bob situation, how was your day?"

We spent an hour there together. Charlie napped in my purse at my feet while Chris and I chatted away. Something about him was comforting. The stress of the investigation melted away as we ate our way through several pounds of crab and shrimp. By the end of the meal, I was stuffed, and we strolled out of the Crab Shack hand in hand, content.

As the cold air of the night hit my skin, the weight of the investigation settled back over my shoulders.

Chris pulled me into a hug and kissed the top of my head. "Thank you for the reprieve. I'm ready for the update."

I buried my head in his shoulder. "I need access to the crime scene."

He rubbed his hand up and down my spine. "We can stop there on the way back to my place, if you want."

I nodded and stepped back. We walked to our cars, and I followed his SUV to the old sheriff's station. The dumpster was still in the parking lot. The streetlight was out, leaving the area in darkness. I squinted up at the building, unable to make out the top floor. I shivered as I exited the car to retrieve my protective gear from the trunk. Most of the mold remediation had been completed on the first floor, but I didn't want to take any chances. I suited up and handed Chris an extra respirator mask I had on hand, just in case. I turned on a heater I'd bought for the car and left Charlie just out of sight in the back seat. I didn't have protective gear for a cat, and I didn't want him breathing in any mold.

Chris led the way into the building, carrying a handheld lantern. He held it overhead as he walked forward. It was too bright to look at directly, so I stared at his feet as we made our way through the building. It was eerie inside, with all the drywall and insulation removed from the first few rooms. As we walked, I relaxed my eyes and willed myself to see the unseen. The green tendril that I'd followed to Beau's body still wound its way through the building. It stopped a few feet short of where it had ended before. The end of it was slowly unraveling since the body had been moved. Within a few weeks, the line might dissipate all together.

"Now what?" Chris asked.

"I do some magic." I dropped my witch's kit on the floor.

Chris held his hand up and quickly checked the room to make sure it had been cleared. The small plastic cones they used to mark evidence had been collected before we arrived. He nodded and stepped back against the wall to give me space.

I pulled out some supplies. I placed a few candles around the room and lit them as I mumbled words to a protective spell. My motes of light swirled around the room then settled into the wood. The room glowed as I walked the space. I started by touching the inside of the wall. The emotions there were muted. No one had touched that area since the wall went up. Some fatigue lingered on the drywall. I shook my hand out and touched a few more areas. The emotions around the room were all pretty much the same. The crime that had happened there had long been covered up by feelings of boredom, which wasn't unexpected for a storage room. Very few exciting things happened in storage rooms.

I grabbed my obsidian mirror next. With it, I could purposefully activate my Sight. It let me glimpse things in the past, but finding anything useful was very hit-or-miss. I held it up to my eye and murmured the words to the spell. Much like the boredom of the walls, the past was just as boring in the mirror. Flickers of people moving boxes or filing paperwork swam across the glass. I chewed on my lip as I slowly spun in place, checking every corner of the space. Nothing stood out.

Frowning, I glanced at the hole in the wall. If I had a chance of seeing something useful, it would be from inside there. My skin crawled at the idea of climbing into a wall. I had climbed into walls before as an adjuster and never found the experience pleasant. They were always cramped, and I couldn't tell if the sensation of something crawling across my skin was a spider, my hair, or pieces of loose insulation or other building material. I swallowed and crawled inside.

My body became heavy. I sank to the floor, my head turning toward the room. I struggled to keep my hand up as I looked into the glass. Boots were a few feet away. They moved. My eyes couldn't focus on them. Everything was so blurry. I wanted to close my eyes and go to sleep as another set of boots came into view, then a third, but the third pair were brown-and-white saddle dress shoes. My chest tightened at the sight of the shoes. Voices murmured. A wet, cloying scent filled my nose. *Mud?* But under that, barely noticeable, was something sweet and almost buttery, like a croissant. I breathed in deeply, trying to remember the scents. I strained my ears, trying to hear what was being said, but everything was out of focus. *Why can't I keep my eyes open?*

I jolted upright as I dropped the mirror.

I scrambled out of the hole and hugged my arms to my body, trying to control the trembling. As I dropped the mirror, I'd felt it—the moment Beau died. He was still alive when they shoved him in there. He hadn't lasted long. He died before the wall was finished. He was too out of it to feel any pain. But it was still so disconcerting. *How could people be so cruel?*

Chris crossed the room and crouched next to me. He put a hand on my shoulder. "Are you okay?"

I shook my head. "It was awful."

"What did you see?" he asked.

I grabbed on to him and sank into his arms as I described it.

"Something sweet?" Chris asked.

I nodded. "So... about that case update. Beau used to have a business partner. They had a falling out."

"Who?"

"Frankie."

Chris tensed. I could feel him shaking his head. I pulled back to look at him as he stood up.

"Frankie is the best man I know," Chris said.

"I know." I stood and wrapped my arms around him. "But I still need to talk to him."

Chris relaxed into my arms, his head resting against mine. "Okay. I'll set something up."

We stood there for a few more minutes in silence. The weight of everything was almost too much to bear. But at least I had Chris, and he had me. After we both calmed down, I collected my candles, and we left, hand in hand.

I still couldn't believe Frankie could've had anything to do with it. But I couldn't ignore that dots that were leading toward him. I just hoped, for Chris's sake, that he was only a witness.

CHAPTER 13

The bed was empty when I woke up. I reached across to Chris's side, and it was cold. He'd been up for a while. I groaned and climbed out of bed. Charlie was nowhere to be seen. I closed my eyes and felt for him. He was downstairs. He was content at being scratched on a good spot on his butt. I smiled lazily and walked into the bathroom to shower. Chris's bathroom was one of my favorite rooms in the house. He had a large jacuzzi tub that was probably big enough for two people. I hummed to myself as I went through the motions of getting ready for the day. I had lunch plans with the Retirees at noon, but before then, I had to do paperwork for my day job. I was in no rush to get to my office to stare at my computer for a few hours. It was going to be hard to focus on. I felt strange that as my life was crumbling around me, I still had to go in to work. But I had to, if I wanted to still have a life when I got to the other side of this investigation—if I got to the other side of it.

I dressed in simple jeans and an oversized sweatshirt then opened the bedroom door to go downstairs. Voices floated up to me from the living room. I froze, my hand gripping the door frame, my ears straining to make them out. They were two men. I exhaled. For a moment, I'd been afraid one of the Wardens had broken in again. The scent of bacon hit me next, followed by something sweeter. *Maple syrup?*

I made my way downstairs and found Chris in the kitchen, making breakfast. Seated at the small dinette was Frankie. His gray hair was clipped short, and he was dressed in a long-sleeved shirt and khaki pants. He stood when I entered the room and stepped around the table to pull out a seat.

"Dani! So good to see you. I hope you don't mind," Frankie said. His voice sounded as I remembered it, a smooth baritone that made me picture him bursting into song at any second. "Chris messaged me this morning, asking to set up a meeting. My morning was free, so I came on over. I've been itching to hear how things are going between you two."

He pushed my seat in and sat back down.

"Things have been great." I smiled up at Chris as he set a coffee mug down in front of me.

"Wonderful. I always thought you two were going to get together."

I ducked my head. In high school, we'd spent hours at his counter. I was too wrapped up in my own head back then to notice how wonderful Chris was. But late was better than never.

"So, what did you want to talk to me about?"

I stared at my hands. The mood in the room was so light and happy that I hated to burst the bubble. "I wanted you to tell me about Beau."

Frankie leaned away from me. "I'm sorry, dear. Who?"

He was still touching the table. I could sense his tension through the wood. He knew exactly who I was talking about. I looked up and held his gaze. "Beau Lancaster. His body was found recently. And your name came up when I asked around about who might have known him."

I couldn't tell if the pain in my chest was from me or him. He stared me straight in the eye as emotions warred inside him. They flickered from shock to grief to guilt and back again. Finally, he settled on a despair that made my vision blur with tears, and my limbs felt like they weighed a thousand pounds. I swallowed, trying to clear the lump in my throat.

Frankie blinked and looked away. "Booker was a fool. A charming fool but a fool nonetheless. He cost me a lot. And never apologized for it. God, I miss him."

"What did he do?" I asked.

"He came back from the war with ideas about how things could change. It was almost like he was playing chicken with the world. Like if he ignored the stares and just kept on doing whatever he wanted, that... that people would give up and leave him alone. But it wasn't just him they stared at. It wasn't just him they hounded. When I first opened Frankie's, he was supposed to be a silent partner, but he couldn't stay quiet about anything. He blabbed, and the next thing I knew, we had rocks thrown through our windows. We lost our lease."

He wouldn't look at me while he spoke. His voice was thick with emotion, somehow angry and despondent at the same time. I stayed quiet and just watched him. There was more, and he needed space to open up.

Frankie wiped at his eyes and glanced at Chris, who hadn't moved from the kitchen behind me. "I tried to do all the right things. I filed a police report. It got lost. Hardly anyone wanted to rent to me until after he disappeared. And even then, the harassment continued. People just wouldn't let it go."

"When did it stop?" I asked.

"When I got to Washington Street."

"Is that when you let Beau's sister go?"

He scrunched his face and turned away. His shoulders

shook. "She was a good kid, but everyone has a breaking point. I kept her on for five years. I didn't want to give up my dream forever."

I stood up and walked around the table. I put my hand on his shoulder. He hid his face from me.

"I always suspected he hadn't just disappeared. I was such a coward."

"Do you know who did it?"

He shook his head. "I know his lady friend had a jealous ex, but he never did tell me who it was. I couldn't prove anything, so I kept quiet."

I squeezed his shoulder and let him cry. Frankie didn't have anything to do with it. Something about his grief was raw. I stood there silently, torn between giving him support and turning my back on him. As I grew up, he'd taught my friend group a lot about loyalty and friendship. That all felt like a lie now. I'd ripped off the mask of my childhood hero and discovered he wasn't as strong as I thought he was. *Did Beau even have any real friends?* I blinked back tears. *Five years is a long time to struggle. Am I being too hard on him?* I clenched my teeth. No, I would never have abandoned Heather like that. I would have stuck by her side always.

Chris emerged from the kitchen with a platter of food. He faltered when he saw my sour expression. He cleared his throat and continued into the room. "Did I tell you how your s'more donut recipe won this girl over?"

Frankie wiped his eyes and smiled. "It did?"

Chris and I sat down at the dinette. Chris started passing out the food as he talked. "An over-twenty-year plan in the making. It wouldn't have been the same without your contributions. It happened just over a week ago."

I leaned back in my chair and ate the bacon Chris had prepared as he launched into the story about how we finally became a couple. With him telling it, the magical evening was even more beautiful. With each word, the anguish that had settled over the table eased up until Frankie was laughing along. I did my best to smile too. I didn't want to make breakfast any more awkward. At the end of the meal, Frankie gathered his things, thanked us for a wonderful meal, and departed. I nestled under Chris's arm as we watched him walk away to his car.

"Thank you," I said.

"Did you get what you needed?"

I nodded.

Chris kissed the top of my head. "Do I want to know?"

"Probably not."

"I was hoping you weren't going to say that." He sighed and held me tight. "Tell me anyway."

CHAPTER 14

I dragged myself into the Slice of Life Diner just after the lunch rush to meet the Retirees. The paperwork had taken longer than expected at work, and I had to push our meal plans back an hour. Charlie was in my purse again, his head poking out to take in our surroundings as we crossed the room. My shoulder ached from carrying him. He hadn't been pleased when I put the harness on him again that morning. As much as he enjoyed his excursions into town with me, he also liked to lounge around the house. This constantly-on-the-go thing was wearing on him, so he refused to walk and wanted me to carry him in my bag from location to location. I set my bag down in the booth and scooted him between me and Sarah.

Betty pushed a coffee across the table toward me. "Looks like you could use a pick-me-up."

I sipped it gratefully as I filled them in on what had transpired the day before. "Have you guys found anything yet?" I asked.

Sarah shook her head.

"We're still going through boxes," Agnes said.

Betty tilted her head back. "Remind me to declutter when

this is all said and done. If I have to look through another box of random odds and ends, I'm going to lose my mind."

Sarah huffed. "It's important memorabilia."

Betty raised her eyebrow and glowered.

Agnes stirred her tea and sipped.

"It is!" Sarah exclaimed.

"Says the hoarder of the group," Betty grumbled and looked away.

I finished the coffee and caught Willow's eye by holding up the cup. "It was a long shot anyway."

Willow made her way over to the table with a coffeepot and topped me up. "Was Donna able to help you?"

"Donna was great," I said.

"That isn't a yes." Willow tapped her foot.

I grimaced. "Yeah. I didn't find what I needed."

"What are you looking for?"

"I'll know it when I see it."

Willow perked up. "Maybe I have it. I went through a box of photos last night while I was watching TV to see if I could find a picture of Beau. I found one. Do you still want to see it?"

As she said the words *found one,* the hairs on the back of my neck stood up. I suppressed a shiver and nodded.

"Be right back." Willow twirled away from the table, her maxi dress billowing around her legs as she glided across the room.

"Don't you already know what he looks like?" Agnes asked.

"I do." I glanced at the door Willow had disappeared through. "But something feels important about this one."

Betty's eyes lit up. My feelings were rarely wrong.

Willow walked back to the table with a photo in hand. She handed it to me. My skin tingled as I looked down at the photo. It was of Beau. He was sitting on top of a car, a wide smile on his face, holding a pair of keys in front of himself.

Behind him was a house I recognized. It was where one of the other green tendrils had ended. I flipped the photo over. In neat black pen were the words:

Booker Lancaster
New Homeowner
October 1st, 1945

"Can I borrow this?" I whispered.

Willow looked over as another patron held up a glass to get her attention. "Sure thing." She left me with the photo.

My hands shook as I handed it to Betty. "It's his house."

The bell above the door jingled. I shuddered as an alarm blared in my head. *Someone's trying to read my thoughts.* I spun in my seat to face the door. Delaney and her associate stood there, staring straight at me.

They didn't waste any time. They strode across the room, Delaney wearing her form-fitting black pants and bright-red top and her associate in her floor-length navy-blue robe. Betty shoved the photo into her pocket and smiled warmly at them as they stopped a foot from the table.

"Danielle Williams, it is time that you came with us." The woman's voice was crisp. She had a transatlantic accent, making her origins difficult to place. She stared down her nose at me, her mouth a thin straight line. It wasn't a request —it was a demand.

Betty hopped out of the booth and stepped between us. "Her schedule is full for the day already. But I've got some free time."

The woman ground her teeth.

"You just need to talk to a coven member, right? Well, coven member reporting as requested." Betty smiled sweetly at them.

Delaney returned the smile, but it didn't reach her eyes as

she placed a hand on her associate's shoulder. "For today, we will let this refusal slide."

My mouth went dry as the woman reached for Betty's arm.

Betty shrugged her off. "Let me say goodbye to my friends first."

They stepped back half a foot and watched as Betty pulled Agnes into a hug. Betty hugged me next. With one arm wrapped around me, she used the other to shove the photo into my hands. "I'll stall as long as I can to buy you more time," Betty murmured.

"Thank you." I slipped the photo into my coat.

I stood there, staring daggers into the Wardens' backs as they led Betty away. I didn't like how the more serious looking of the two kept her hand on Betty's shoulder until they disappeared out the front door.

Deflating, I collapsed into the booth behind me. Charlie stuck his head out of my purse and chirped for me. I mindlessly scratched his head until the tension in my neck eased up.

"How long do you think they'll have her?" I asked.

Agnes shrank in on herself. "I don't know. But we should let Megan know they're making the rounds more forcefully now."

"I'll go out to the farm," Sarah offered.

"I'll keep looking through the boxes." Agnes sighed.

I collected my bag and scooted out of the booth. "And I'll try to find answers before they come and grab another one of us."

I gripped the steering wheel so tightly that my knuckles went white. At moments, deep in my investigation of Beau's murder, I could almost forget that the Wardens were in town, trying to track down my daughter. While finding out what happened to Beau, for the sake of justice, was important, figuring out how it connected to the curse and my daughter's possession mattered more. I couldn't stop until I found the truth.

I parked my car across the street from Beau's house. I pulled out the photo and glanced between it and what was there presently. It had been updated. The windows were new, and the small sycamore tree in the front yard had grown from a baby in the photo to an impressive eighty-foot tree, its branches arching over the whole yard and most of the roadway. The home was a beautiful brick structure in an older part of town. It wasn't far from Benjamin Hayes's house.

Icy wind bit into my skin as I climbed out of the car. I leaned against the driver's-side door and stared up at the building. *What now?* I stamped my feet to stay warm and thrust my hands under my arms. When I left the diner, I hadn't fully thought through my plan. It ended with me arriving at the house, then the plan stopped. I'd come on instinct, half expecting to find something important on the doorstep.

As I stared at the front door, it swung inward. A man carrying a large cardboard box stepped out and walked toward a midsize black SUV parked in the driveway. He fumbled with it, shoving it into the back seat before retrieving a thermos from inside the vehicle. He was turning back toward the house when he spotted me. I raised my hand and waved.

Wringing my hands in front of me, I approached. "Good morning."

"The open house isn't until next week," he said.

"Oh, I wasn't here about that." I smiled and brushed a loose strand of hair behind my ear. "This might sound like an odd question, but how much do you know about the home?"

"A fair amount." He sipped from his thermos. "I've lived here my whole life. Although I have to admit I've never really cared for it. It meant the world to my father, and we didn't exactly get along."

I blinked and opened my mouth. I wasn't sure how to respond to that.

"Sorry, where are my manners?" He held out his hand. "I'm Kevin. I apologize. I'm a bit frazzled this week. I'm here managing my father's estate for my brother and me. I'm trying to prep the place to sell."

"I'm sorry. My condolences for your loss."

He waved his hand and sipped something from his thermos again. "Thanks, but that's unnecessary. Why are you asking about the house if you're not here to buy it?"

"I'm interested in a former owner. Do you know when your dad bought the place?"

"Well, before he had me. Sometime in the forties, I think."

I licked my lips to moisten them. "Do you know who he bought it from? Was it Booker Lancaster?"

He frowned and shook his head. "I don't think so. Although Lancaster sounds vaguely familiar. Booker, you said?"

I smiled and quickly mumbled the words to the relaxation spell under my breath. Motes of light flew straight to his thermos as he raised it back to his lips to take another sip. Within seconds, the glow of the spell had settled into his skin. "He also went by the name Beau."

Kevin snapped his fingers and pointed at me. "I remember now. I must have been, like, eight at the time. Jim and Harold were over. They had this massive fight. Jim kept screaming that he lied to him about Beau. He was tired of being used. He was drunk as a skunk, but they were never the same after that fight. They still always came over but never together."

I tried to gauge his age. He looked well over a decade

older than me, which would have put the fight in the seventies or early eighties at the latest. *Was he remembering it right?* I couldn't risk that he wasn't. "They sound like colorful characters. I'd love to hear more about them."

"Sure." He gestured for me to follow him. "Cleaning out this old house has me feeling nostalgic."

I followed him into the house. It was crowded with half-filled boxes. He led me to the dining room and rifled through some frames.

He pulled out a photo and handed it to me. "My dad was part of this old boys' club. That's him there." He pointed at a thin, wiry man standing at the edge of the group. "His name was Thomas. And that is Harold, his brother Jim, Uncle Benji, and George."

I took in every detail of the photo. Looking at them was odd. Benji was a much younger Benjamin Hayes. I recognized his hook nose. Harold and Jim looked similar, but Jim was much broader in the shoulders. Harold had a coat hanging over his shoulders. They looked vaguely familiar. But when my eyes landed on George's face, I froze. He was much younger, but somehow, he was still a spitting image of his son, Robert Wright, the sheriff.

Kevin's phone rang in his pocket. He peeked at it, held up a finger, and stepped away to take the call. I glanced at his back and quickly pulled out my own phone to take a picture of the photo. I slipped it out of the frame and turned it over. It said 1946 in one corner. They were all young and vibrant. I took a photo of the back and slipped the picture back into the frame before Kevin turned back around.

"I'm sorry, but I've gotta go. My client's case got bumped up to this afternoon's docket."

"You're an attorney?"

He smiled sheepishly. "Just like the old man. Except I went into family law instead of real estate."

I handed back the photo. "Maybe another time."

"I'll be here all week. Stop by again if you want to hear me ramble some more."

I shoved my hands into my pockets and trudged out to my car. Charlie was waiting for me, curled up on his heated cat bed in the back seat. I stared at the photo, zooming in on the feet. Jim wore boots, but the other men all had saddle shoes on. Unfortunately, the photo was in black-and-white, so I couldn't tell what color they were. I studied their faces. The truth settled into my chest. I knew it with every fiber of my being.

"One of you killed Beau. But which one?"

I had one potential witness left to question. I hoped Johnny Foster would know.

CHAPTER 15

I arrived at the Crab Shack as Martha was unlocking the doors. I hovered behind her, shifting my weight from foot to foot as she turned on the propane heaters for the exterior seating and flipped the sign on the door to Open.

She glanced back at me as she went about setting up the hostess stand. "You here for Johnny?"

"Is he back from his fishing trip yet?"

She nodded. "Got back at midday. He's cleaning his squid out back on the deck just off the kitchen."

I glanced over her shoulder at the kitchen.

She shook her head, smiling. "Must be a really good ghost story for you to be so on edge. Go on back."

I thanked her and scurried past. I followed the back wall of the kitchen to the exterior door that said Emergency Exit in red paint. It sat ajar, letting saltwater air drift in from Puget Sound. The sun was setting as I stepped out onto the deck. Rickety stairs to one side led down to the wave-beaten beach below, where a small table sat with rusted folding chairs around it. Johnny Foster was sitting at the table, a bucket of fish guts at his feet and a cooler of freshly caught squid waiting to be processed next to him on a chair. His face was a mass of wrinkles and sun-worn skin.

He smiled at me, his brown eyes comforting. "I don't see any hot cocoa in your hands."

I laughed. "I can go get some if that's the price of a good story."

He shook his head. "It probably wouldn't go well with the fish-guts smell anyway. Ghost stories do, though. Which one did you want to hear? By the way Martha spoke, it sounded like you had a specific one in mind."

I took a seat across from him. The beat-up chair groaned under my weight, but it held. I shifted forward slightly so that I could quickly stand if it changed its mind. "I was hoping to hear the one about Beau."

"I was hoping you would want to hear a fun one." He sliced and cleaned the squid and slid the waste into the bucket at his feet. "Are you sure you want that cautionary old tale?"

"It's important."

He grunted and moved on to cleaning the next squid. His movements were quick and precise. He'd been a fisherman longer than I had been alive. "I suppose you could say it's a variation on the boy who cried wolf. The story starts in the fall. The great war has ended. The streets are filled with soldiers back from the Pacific. And there's a young boy who just wants to make a little money so he can buy himself a walkie-talkie to talk to his friends, so he takes odd jobs running errands around town."

I rested a hand on the table. He didn't touch it often enough to get a consistent read, but whenever he did, I got the sour taste of defeat in my mouth.

"This boy, though, he had a bedtime, which he was always missing for this reason or that. Every time he crawled through his window, trying to sneak back in, his mama would catch him and say, 'Where have you been, little one?'" When he quoted the mother, he softened his voice. It came out singsong, but somehow still stern and disappointed. It was the perfect imitation of a mother tired from chasing children all day. "And every time, the boy made up some fanciful story about breaking up a bar fight or saving another little kid from drowning. It got to the point that when his mama would tuck him in, she would listen to his stories like they were bedtime tales."

My breath escaped my throat. I hadn't realized I'd been holding it. Behind his words, melancholy was mixed with acceptance.

He reached for another squid. "One night, the boy was running late again. He was already planning what tale he would spin when he got home, and he heard something up ahead: angry voices and a fearful one. The sounds were getting closer. And closer. The boy decided to hide. He jumped behind a trash can behind the old corner store and watched. Beau, known for his beauty, or so the boy thought, ran through the streets as a car chased him. Have you ever tried to win a footrace against a car?"

I shook my head.

"It went about as well as could be expected. Beau didn't win. Someone from the vehicle hit Beau with a bat as they drove by. And Beau went down like a sack of potatoes. And then the largest of the group got out, picked Beau up like he weighed nothing at all, and carted him away. Scared, the boy ran all the way home. That night, he didn't climb in through his window. He ran straight through the front door. But his mama still looked at him and said those words, 'Where have you been, little one?'"

He must have been hit in the head. That's why he was so groggy in my vision. I swallowed, trying to forget how heavy my limbs had felt when I was inside the wall.

"The little boy told his mama what he saw, but she just

put him to bed like it was any other night. You see, she had heard so many tall tales from him that the truth had been eaten by all of his lies."

"What did the boy do then?" I asked.

He looked up at me. "I usually stop at the lesson learned."

"It's important," I said.

He nodded and grabbed another squid. "He wouldn't let it go. He got out of bed again and again until his mama finally agreed to go to the neighbor's house to call the sheriff. But the sheriff wouldn't believe him either. He said if someone had been attacked like that, there would be a body or signs of a struggle. And the boy's mama put him back to bed again."

I pulled out my phone and opened the photo I'd taken of the picture at Kevin's house. I turned my phone around so that he could see it. "Were these the men the boy saw?"

Johnny studied my face for a second before looking at the phone. He leaned forward, his face scrunched up in concentration. He nodded and pointed. "That one right there. That's the one who carried Beau away." He pointed straight at Jim.

I swallowed. "Were any of the others there?"

"Both of the Mitchell boys. And two of their friends. All of them except for George." He turned back to his squid.

"Mitchell boys?"

"Harold and Jim Mitchell."

Their names were familiar. I had encountered their names on a prior case then heard them again recently—not just from Kevin but somewhere else. I just couldn't remember where. I pursed my lips and sat back.

"The boy did see George that night, though. He was the deputy who came to the boys' house."

I nodded and murmured my thanks. My legs shook as I made my way off the deck and back through the kitchen. I walked in a daze past Martha. The case had just gotten even more complicated. No body, no crime—the body was found inside the wall of the station house. If he put it there, he would have known the body wouldn't be found. It sure sounded like George Wright, the current sheriff's father, helped cover up a murder. *And how on earth am I going to prove that?* Almost everyone in town knew Bob and I didn't get along. *Will they think I'm leaping to conclusions?* Am *I leaping to conclusions?* I grumbled as I climbed into my car and headed back to Chris's. I needed a sounding board who knew both of us well enough to see things clearly.

I drove straight to Chris's townhome. His SUV was already parked in the driveway. I squeezed my car in next to his and let myself in. I found Chris in the kitchen, brushing butter on top of two pot pies. My mouth watered at the faint scent of garlic that wafted through the air. I walked up behind him, wrapped my arms around his waist, and pressed my face into his back.

"Feeling lazy tonight. Hope you don't mind something super simple for dinner," he said over his shoulder.

"You're so good to me," I mumbled.

I released him and made my way into the living room to wait. I curled up on the couch. Charlie jumped out of my purse, stretched, and flopped down next to me. The little stinker had napped most of the day and was still yawning. I scratched him under his chin until Chris joined us. I melted into Chris's side, curling up against him as he wrapped his arm around my shoulder. "How was your day?"

I burrowed in deeper to his side. "Difficult. I think I've narrowed down the suspect pool. But it's... complicated."

"Isn't it always?"

Sighing, I sat up. I quickly updated him on the case. I was building to mentioning George's name when Chris cut me off. "*The* Harold Mitchell?"

I raised my eyebrow. "I guess. I thought he was some sort

of wealthy businessman. But by the way you said *the,* I'm assuming there's more to it than that."

"He's the closest Point Pleasant has to a mobster."

My laugh died in my throat when Chris's expression shifted to a serious one.

"Nothing ever stuck. His family rose to prominence during the Great Depression. He and his brother bought up half of downtown with the money they inherited from their father's rum running. When he took over from his dad, all their rivals sort of disappeared."

I swallowed. "Like Beau did? There isn't still organized crime in Point Pleasant. Is there?"

Chris stroked my shoulder with his thumb. "No. Jim went legit in the fifties and became a respected businessman in the area. In theory, Harold did too. But there was still a lot of questionable stuff around his dealings until he retired in the eighties. He probably never fully left his criminal past in the past. The community back then looked the other way because of all his charitable donations. And now... he's just a lonely old man who rarely leaves his house."

"And Thomas Reynolds, he was their lawyer?"

"Yeah. He started as a defense attorney but ended up in real estate law."

"Odd transition," I said.

"He shifted focus when his clients shifted focus."

I chewed on my lip. *With Thomas dead, did Harold need a new lawyer? Or was he as retired as Chris claimed?*

"What are you thinking?" Chris asked.

"How much do you know about Kevin Reynolds?"

"Not much. He doesn't do defense work. I've only crossed his path when I've had to deal with CPS. He does a lot of custody cases. I remember hearing he does a lot of pro bono work for single moms. He seemed like a good dude."

No new lawyer, then. At least not through Kevin anyway. Maybe the brother? Or he really could be retired. I shifted on the love seat, stalling. Saying George Wright's name was like opening a can of worms. I exhaled, closed my eyes, and grimaced as the words left my mouth. "I think George Wright might have helped keep Harold out of trouble."

Chris stilled next to me. I opened one eye, peeking at his face. His expression was impassive, but through the couch, I could feel the swirling emotions inside. Shock warred with denial and curiosity. He opened his mouth to speak a few times before standing and pacing. Finally, he turned to me, resignation in his eyes. "I never worked for George. Bob practically hero-worshipped the guy. If it's true, it's going to destroy him."

Bob didn't like me much, and the feeling was mutual.

I set that aside and kept my tone neutral. "Do you think he would hide it if it's true?"

Chris shook his head. "Bob is a lot of things, but a dirty cop isn't one of them."

I stood and joined him in the middle of the room. I reached out and took his hand, peering up into his face. "You know I have to keep pushing, right?"

"I do."

"Is that going to be a problem for you?"

"I don't know." He squeezed my hand. "But I'll deal with it. I just hope you find what you're looking for sooner rather than later."

I stepped in and wrapped my arms back around him, pulling him into a hug. "Needing your personal space already, huh?"

Chris chuckled and kissed me on the top of my head. "You staying here has been wonderful. But I can tell you don't feel whole without Grace around. And I really hope that we can bring her back home together."

Home. I smiled and closed my eyes. He was right that I didn't feel whole without Grace. But part of me did feel at home there. Having something to hold on to while I was adrift was nice. Having him in my corner anchored me. Next, all I had to figure out was who'd wielded the bat and how I could tie the case to them, all without destroying the life of someone I didn't like but probably wasn't a bad man. Simple enough. I would just have to sleep on it, hoping an idea would come to me in the morning.

CHAPTER 16

By the time I woke up the next morning, an idea of how to proceed hadn't manifested. I didn't have long to dwell, though, because five minutes after I woke up, Sarah texted me two words that made my heart ache: "Betty's home." In the back of my mind, I'd felt her while the Wardens held her for over a day. She was tired and annoyed but never in pain. My heart ached. They held her because they were trying to get to my daughter through me, and she had stepped in.

DANI:
Is she okay?

SARAH:
She claims to be fine. She wants a case update, so she knows her noble sacrifice was worthwhile.

I raised an eyebrow at the word "noble." *Is Sarah being sarcastic? Betty could be dramatic at times, but I would be, too, if the Wardens questioned me for that long.*

DANI:
Meet me at the Bizzy Bean.

I quickly showered and dressed. Charlie tried to hide under the bed, objecting to another straight day of being put into his harness.

"You'll get to see Star," I promised him.

He poked his head out. Star was his mother and a permanent resident at the Bizzy Bean Cafe. She acted as foster mom to all the kittens who came through Heather's door. Charlie adored his mom. He crept out and let me put his harness on him, but he still grumbled through the bond. If Star wasn't out and about, I was sure he was going to revolt.

The Retirees were already at our usual table when I arrived. Megan pulled up in her pickup truck thirty seconds behind me, and we walked in together. Charlie trotted ahead of me as we made our way through the cat enclosure on the left. Heather finished up behind the counter and ducked out to meet us, leaving her barista Becca in charge. As I took my seat, Star poked her head out from inside the cat castle that took up most of the far-left wall. I let Charlie off his leash, and he launched himself across the room to go play.

I watched him scamper about as Heather dropped coffees in front of each of us then finally claimed a seat next to me. We sat in silence while Agnes cast her usual protection spell to prevent eavesdropping. She finished the spell by sprinkling salt around the table in a circle.

"Are you okay?" I asked Betty.

She nodded. I could sense how tired she was, but intermixed with it was a feeling of triumph. Betty was proud of herself.

"They questioned me for hours. I think I annoyed them with how long-winded I could be in my responses."

I reached across the table and squeezed her hand. "Thank you."

"Now I'm starving." Betty turned to Heather. "You still got any of those triple-chocolate muffins?"

Heather nodded and scampered off. She returned,

shoving a plate filled with chocolate muffins, peanut butter cookies, and butter-roasted pecans toward Betty. She swiped a few pieces of salt to the side and wrinkled her nose. "I hope all the salt we've been using doesn't damage the floors."

"Sorry, dear." Agnes winced.

"Is there another substance that you can use instead?" Heather asked.

"In theory, but most of the other things can be a tad dangerous," Agnes began.

Sarah nodded. "The best option is mercury."

"But everyone knows that's toxic," Betty concluded as she broke one of the cookies in two. Her voice cracked as she spoke, and her shoulders were rounded inward. Her exhaustion from her ordeal was written all over her face.

Agnes capped the salt and put it back into her bag. She squeezed Betty's hand in support. "There are some gemstones that could work."

"Crystals, actually," Sarah corrected.

"But you would have to hang them around, so it's impractical for pop-up meetings like this." Betty closed her eyes and sank into the booth. She had a small smile on her lips as she chewed.

Heather smiled. "I have a suspicion these pop-up meetings are going to become routine. Maybe something more permanent would be worth investing in."

I looked around. "You could go with a more New Agey look. Hanging crystals from the ceiling isn't the weirdest thing you've ever done."

Heather laughed. "I would think about adding in some centerpieces, but the cats would have a field day with them."

Megan put a hand on Heather's shoulder. "I can help you come up with some ideas on how to work it into the decor if you would like. Since I've had no social life until recently, I spent way too much time on Pinterest over the years. I've got some good stuff pinned."

Heather nodded.

After everyone was settled in, I launched into the latest update.

"Do you think the other lines end at places connected to Beau's death?" Agnes asked.

"Definitely," I said.

"Let's make sure. That information should all be on the assessor's website, right?" Heather asked.

I pulled out my laptop and typed in each location. We knew where the first two tendrils ended: Beau's old home, presently owned by Kevin Reynolds, and the sheriff's station, where Beau's body had been interred. According to the assessor's records, the other tendrils ended at the homes that Harold Mitchell, Thomas Reynolds, Benjamin Hayes, James Mitchell, and George Wright owned at the time of the murder. The last tendril ended at a home that was a new construction but, back in the 1940s, was a corner store. Based on Johnny's story, that would have been where Beau was mowed down by the car.

I furrowed my brow, looking back over the list. All the locations related to his death. His body. Who may have been responsible. Who may have covered it up. The only place that stood out was Beau's house. It hadn't been bought out until after Beau died. *Did a tendril lead there because of the injustice of that?* I chewed on my lip. An odd sensation was building in my gut that told me that line of thought was wrong. The tendril led there for a reason, and it wasn't because it belonged to Beau. It was because of something else.

"I think I need to go back to Beau's home," I said.

An alarm went off in my head. I froze in place. Someone was trying to read my thoughts again. I glanced up. Agnes was staring past me at the door, a look of barely contained fury on her face. I turned, following her gaze. My eyes landed on Delaney and her associate standing in the doorway, staring at me.

I swallowed as they strode in unison across the room. I was getting tired of their antics, especially since I was so close to finding an answer. They came to a stop in front of me.

"Danielle Williams, it is really time that you come with us," Delaney's associate said.

"I'm busy," I said with more confidence than I really felt.

"Miranda—" Delaney put her hand on her associate's shoulder.

Miranda narrowed her eyes and took a step forward. "Why do you delay? The longer we are here, the longer an Outsider exerts its influence in this region."

"I'll go," Agnes stood up.

Delaney smiled sweetly. Again, it didn't reach her eyes. She reached forward and snaked her hand around Agnes's wrist. "Wonderful. Let's get to know one another."

I sat frozen in my seat as Agnes was frog-marched past me. My heart did somersaults in my chest until the door closed behind them. It was only a matter of time before they came back again. I could delay going with them only so many more times. I had to hurry and find answers before we were too late and they figured out where I was hiding Grace. I grabbed my purse and whistled for Charlie to come to me.

"I've got to go."

The rest of my coven sat in silence as I harnessed Charlie and left. They were doing their best to support me, but finding answers was my responsibility.

CHAPTER 17

I followed my GPS to Kevin's house and parked in the shade of the sycamore tree. The lights were out, and the street was empty. That was unsurprising, given that it was the middle of the workday. Most people would be at their jobs or at school right then. The driveway was empty. I stared at the house, fidgeting in my seat. Charlie chirped at me from the passenger seat. He stood and placed his front paws on the dashboard, staring up at the house with me. I had to get inside. But my stomach had qualms about my breaking in. Every place I'd been during an investigation so far, I had technically been invited to in some capacity. Ish. *Okay. Not everything has been aboveboard so far.* But Chris's insistence on being legal had worn me down. *Maybe I can see something useful through a window.* My hand hovered over the door handle.

Kevin's SUV pulled into the driveway. Charlie jumped into the back seat and lay down on his heated cat bed. The tension in my shoulders released as I pushed my car door open and crossed the street to greet him. "Kevin? Remember me? We met the other day."

He smiled. "Back so soon? I didn't realize the home's

history was so entertaining. What can I help you with today?"

I faltered. My mind went a mile a minute, vacillating back and forth between options on how to answer. Sweet-talking him would be the easiest but would take the longest. If Chris was right, and he was a good guy, maybe the straightforward approach was best. He cocked an eyebrow, waiting for me to respond.

"I'm sorry. I don't know how to say this, so I'm just going to come right out with it. The prior owner of your home was just found buried behind a wall at a construction site. He was murdered in 1945. And... I think your dad's friend Harold Mitchell may have had something to do with it."

He blinked at me, his jaw dropping.

"And if I'm right, your dad knew something. Something that may be helpful in putting all the pieces together."

He ran his hand through his hair and turned away.

I held my breath, waiting for him to say something.

He turned back and dropped his hands to his sides. "Harold isn't a good man."

"I have questions, if you're willing to talk."

He moved away from me, walking up the walkway to the front door. "You might as well come inside. You want some tea? Or something stronger?"

"Tea would be great."

I followed him into the house. He walked ahead of me into the kitchen. I paused at the entryway to relax my eyes and find the green tendril that had entered the house through the front door. It curved to the right and flowed up the stairs.

"I have peppermint or chamomile," Kevin called from the kitchen.

"Peppermint, please." I turned away from the tendril and stepped into the dining room. "How well did you know Harold?"

"About as well as any kid knows their father's friends." He turned the electric kettle on and joined me at the table while the water heated. "His friendship made my father paranoid. *Friendship* might be the wrong word, honestly. Harold came around a lot. They had poker nights. Barbecues on occasion. But I found my dad searching the house for bugs more than once after he left."

"Bugs?"

"Like wiretaps. My dad destroyed more than one phone over the years, looking for them. And the security systems. More than once, he became convinced Harold had figured out how to bypass it, so we got a new one. It was exhausting at times."

I lightly touched the table to get a read on him and found he was tired but sincere. "Why were they still friends, then?"

"The money. Harold was his best-paying client. At times, his only client. They were *friends* out of necessity." He put air quotes around the word *friends*.

"If he was a client, why would your dad be worried about bugs?"

"I don't know." He got up to pour the water kettle as it screeched. "It was a love-hate relationship. My dad couldn't stand the guy but also couldn't stand anyone speaking ill of him."

I tapped my fingers against the table. Thomas had been scared of something. *But why would Harold want to bug the house? Unless...* "Did your dad ever take his work home with him?"

"All the time. He never threw anything out. Most of it's still up in the attic."

I leaned forward in my seat as he carried the steaming mug of tea to me. "Mind if I poke around up there?"

He shrugged and put the mug down. "Sure. But it might be hard to find what you're looking for."

I followed him up two flights of stairs to the attic. He

pushed the door open, revealing a large space that ran the length of the house. It was stacked from floor to rafters with boxes. Narrow paths wound through the towering mess.

I glanced between him and the mess. "This is a lot."

He winced. "I had planned to keep this door locked during the open house. No way am I getting through all of it in a week."

I nodded as I entered the room. He hovered in the doorway behind me as I turned slowly in place, trying to get my bearings. It was a tight space, with only a few inches on either side of me before the walls of boxes began. I exhaled slowly and relaxed my eyes. The green tendril snaked past me into the room. *Jackpot.*

I followed the tendril as best I could through the winding paths. It disappeared from sight a few times, but I managed to refind it. After a few minutes of shuffling through the space, the tendril stopped at a wooden trunk and didn't emerge on the other side. It was a steamer chest with an oversized padlock sealing it shut.

"Did you think you have the keys to this thing?" I asked.

Kevin shuffled through the stacks behind me and peered over my shoulder. "Somewhere."

My heart sank in my chest.

"It would be faster to cut it open. I have bolt cutters downstairs." He disappeared back down the stairs.

While he was gone, I carefully moved boxes around until the chest was clear. On closer inspection, it looked more like a footlocker. It was old. On the side, it said Property of the US Army. I wiped away the last of the dust as Kevin returned with the bolt cutters. He handed them to me and stepped back.

The lock broke easily. I unhooked it and tossed it aside. My hands shook as I lifted the lid. The air inside the footlocker was stale. It was half empty. A long object was wrapped in plastic, and next to it sat a box of photos. My breath caught in my throat as I picked up the first photo. It was of Harold standing over Beau's body with a bat in hand.

"Is that—" Kevin stumbled back. "I think I'm going to be sick." He ran from the room.

I put the photo back and carefully lifted the corner of the plastic. It was the bat. Thomas Reynolds had kept an insurance policy against Harold. That's what he was paranoid about. He was afraid Harold would come to collect it. I closed the lid of the trunk and grabbed my phone. I started babbling the second Chris answered his phone. "I'm going to text you an address. Get here quickly. I've cracked the case wide open." I hung up before he could get a word in, sent the promised message, then stumbled downstairs to find Kevin.

I found him in the dining room. He was sitting slumped, his mug of tea clasped between his hands, and was staring wide-eyed at the wall in shock. I patted him on the shoulder and sat down next to him.

"The police are on their way," I said.

He nodded and sipped his tea.

"There was a bloody man in that photo. Was that... Was that the prior owner?"

I nodded.

"So this house..." He swallowed and gestured around. "It's stolen, isn't it?"

"Probably."

"And my dad... He was okay with it?"

"I don't know." I placed my hand over his.

We sat there like that, in silence, until Chris arrived. Kevin was too stunned to move, so I led Chris up to the pile of evidence. He cursed as he bagged the photos. So many were in there—not just of Beau's murder but others too. And George was in a lot of them. Chris called it in to Peggy, their local dispatch, for backup. I left before they could arrive. I didn't want to be there when Bob had to face the truth. He would probably just add it to the list of reasons he hated me.

I retreated to my car and texted the coven chat.

DANI:
I know who killed Beau. One last update?

HEATHER:
I'll get Becca to cover the register again.

I shoved my phone into my pocket and made my way back to the Bizzy Bean. Megan and Betty's trucks were parked out front. Charlie dashed inside ahead of me. Heather enveloped me in a hug and guided me back to our table, where Sarah and Betty were already waiting. I collapsed into the booth and closed my eyes. I had solved it. But nothing felt different.

"Well?" Heather sat down across from me.

I shook my head. "It was Harold Mitchell. I found the murder weapon. And a boatload of evidence."

"That's great, isn't it?" Megan claimed a chair at the end of the table.

I opened my mouth and closed it. *It is great, isn't it? Why do I still feel so uneasy?* "I think so. But I still don't know how this helps Grace."

"Call Kim," Betty suggested.

Sarah nodded. "Maybe there's been some sort of change."

I pulled my phone out. Kimberly answered on the third ring. It went straight to a Facetime chat. Her phone was propped up and aimed straight into her kitchen. I could see her elbow as she chopped veggies. A pile of potatoes blocked half the screen. "What?"

"How's Grace?" I asked.

"Fine. I just re-upped the sleeping spell. She's going through it faster, which is annoying, by the way. She is down to three days at Casa Jones. You any closer to figuring out how to save her?" She grabbed the potatoes and dropped them into a pot of water.

"Maybe? I found out who killed Meredith's boyfriend." I paused. "Ghosts are supposed to be looking for a resolution, right? An answer? So, maybe... if Meredith didn't know who did it, the answer might make her rest. And if she's resting, then the Outsider doesn't need to be here anymore. It wouldn't be held here by the deal it made with her anymore. And... And... I don't know. I'm grasping at straws. I guess I just assumed it would go away if we resolved what was keeping Meredith here."

Kimberly sprinkled salt into the pot. "Sounds about as good a plan as any."

"Okay." I sat up. "I guess I'll do it, then. I just walk up to Meredith's house. Open the front door and... politely say Harold Mitchell is the one who killed your boyfriend. He's going to be arrested. Eighty years late."

Kimberly grunted again but with a different tone to it. Her face slid into view as she fell to the floor.

"Kimberly?" I clutched my phone. "Kim? Kim, are you okay?"

Grace picked up the phone and smiled at the camera. "I'm not going back to sleep." She hung up.

CHAPTER 18

My chest tightened, and I couldn't breathe. The room spun around me as I tried to stand and run for the door. I didn't make it far before I had to stop and grab on to a table. Spots floated through my vision. Kimberly was in danger because of me. I had asked her to look after Grace. *If she's hurt...* After I stumbled forward a few more steps, hands grabbed me from behind and spun me around. Megan's face swam into view.

"What happened?" By her expression, I could tell that wasn't the first time she'd asked.

I swallowed, my mouth dry. "I have to go."

Sarah and Betty appeared over her shoulder. Megan didn't release her grip. She held my gaze, forcing me to look her in the eye. "What happened?"

"Grace woke up and attacked Kimberly," I croaked.

Megan stepped back and grabbed her bag from the booth. "I'm coming with you."

I looked from Megan to Sarah to Betty, then my gaze settled on Heather. They'd all gathered their purses and were walking toward me. Tears welled in my eyes. I'd never had people I could count on before. I'd already put Kimberly in danger. I didn't know if I could handle putting them in danger, too, and something happening to them. "It isn't safe."

"And that's why we're coming too," Heather said.

My jaw quivered.

"We're in a coven, right?" Heather asked.

I nodded weakly.

"Covens don't let their members face threats alone." Sarah crossed her arms, daring me to deny it.

I turned away from them. Charlie was waiting for me by the entrance. He was staring at the door, his tail swishing. "Not you too, buddy." I could feel his determination through the bond. None of them were going to let me face this alone. *This is all my fault. I shouldn't have taken Grace into Meredith's house. I should have taken better care of her. And now all my friends might suffer. But it's their decision.* I hung my head. *Don't be like gran. Don't take away their choices.* "Fine, but... don't take any unnecessary risks."

Betty power walked past me, holding her keys over her head. "I'm driving."

I gritted my teeth and followed her out. I shoved my hands into my pockets to hide their shaking. It was probably for the best that she drove, but I didn't have to like it. I climbed into the front seat and stared out the passenger's window as she made her way through town to Kimberly's home. I steadied my breathing as she drove, trying to mentally prepare myself for what we might find when we arrived.

Kimberly's house looked exactly like it had the first time I saw it. The lights were on, illuminating pastel curtains that gave the house a cheery, almost welcoming feel. The hair on the back of my neck stood up, and the pressure at the back of my head pulsed, screaming danger. I swallowed, wetting my lips. Finally outside the house, I wasn't sure if I was actually ready to go in.

Heather climbed out first and strode toward the front

door. I scrambled out of the car. "I said no unnecessary risks," I hissed at her as I caught up with her.

"I knew you would be right behind me." She held out a hand.

I grabbed it, and we continued together up the pathway. The rest of the coven clustered in behind me when I came to a stop outside the front door. It stood ajar by about half an inch. I pushed the door open.

It was quiet inside. The only sounds were the hum of electricity from the overhead lights. Cautiously, I stepped into the house. I paused just through the doorway, straining my ears to hear. *Nothing.* I inched my way forward through the living room and poked my head around the corner to see into the kitchen. Kimberly lay sprawled across the floor, her crutches just out of reach. Her eyes were closed, and she was breathing shallowly.

Nothing jumped out at me. The hair on my arms and neck relaxed. Grace wasn't there.

I walked into the kitchen and turned off the stove so that the potato water wouldn't boil over then kneeled to check on Kimberly. I unfocused my eyes. Green sparkles floated around her head. It looked almost identical to the magic Megan had used on Grace. "She's under a sleeping spell."

Megan crouched next to me, her hands hovering over Kimberly's head. She murmured something under her breath, and translucent red petals floated out of her mouth. The petals glided down and sank into Kimberly's skin. Kimberly gasped, sputtered, and pushed herself up to a sitting position.

"Are you okay?" Megan whispered.

"Like you care." Kimberly turned away. She held her hand out behind herself. "My crutches."

I reached over to grab one, but Megan beat me to it. She held them, almost tenderly, before placing them in Kimberly's waiting hand.

"Did you break anything?" Megan asked as Kimberly heaved herself up from the ground.

"No." Kimberly patted her pockets. "She took my keys."

I stepped back into the living room and peered out at the driveway. It had been drizzling on and off all day. I'd missed it when we pulled up, but a section of driveway was dry, where a car had been not too long before. *Shoot.* "She has your car. What does it look like? Do you have a photo?"

"On my phone, probably." Kimberly hunched her shoulders and moved past Megan, who was hovering awkwardly in the kitchen. Heather, Betty, and Sarah stood in the living room, looking on, as Kimberly retrieved her phone and found a photo. Kimberly shoved it toward me before collapsing into a chair at the dinette table.

I stared at the photo on her phone and pulled out my own. She couldn't have gotten far. I pulled up my maps app and zoomed out to show the surrounding area. With Kimberly's phone in one hand, my phone in the other, I whispered the words to a tracking spell. Golden motes of light swirled between Kimberly's phone and my own. They didn't settle on the screen. They slowly moved across it along a street not too far away. I recognized the street name. It was the road Harold lived on.

Shoot. I texted myself the photo of her car. "She's on the move. I think she's going to Harold's."

"For revenge?" Heather asked.

"Why else?" I stared at the dot as it came to a stop outside his house. "We've got to stop her. I can't let whatever's possessing her make her into a killer."

"Dani." Megan reached toward me. "I hate to suggest it, but maybe it's time to call in the Wardens. This feels bigger than what we can handle on our own."

"She's right." Betty nodded.

"After what they did to you?" Sarah gaped.

"They asked a lot of questions, but they weren't exactly

rough about it. Just... overly insistent." Betty crossed her arms.

"For now." Sarah put her hands on her hips. "We've heard the stories."

I shoved my phone into my pocket. "I don't care right now. Call them. Don't. I don't have time to stop and think. Grace is already there. I have to leave. Now."

Megan nodded and stepped up beside me. "Then let's go."

"Typical." Kimberly spat.

Megan froze.

"It's just like you to take off as soon as I'm wounded and vulnerable. Have you ever thought she might come back?"

"I..." Megan floundered. "I didn't think you would want me to stay."

Kimberly shifted in her seat until she was facing away from us all. Her shoulders shook. "You're always leaving me."

Megan looked between me and Kimberly, her expression helpless. She stepped away from me and crouched down in front of her. "I never wanted to go. I thought you wanted space. So I gave it to you."

"Typical," Kimberly croaked.

"What's typical?" Megan asked.

"You're so used to rejection you rejected yourself first." Kimberly wiped at her eyes.

"The coven broke up. What was I supposed to think?" Megan stood, her gaze bouncing between me and Kimberly.

"I have to go now, Megan. You don't have to come if you're needed here," I said.

"I'll stay." Heather stepped into the room.

We all turned to her, stunned.

"It took all of you to capture Grace last time. You'll need all the help you can get. So Megan can't stay here. She has to be with you. But I'm not going to be much help there. I've got no magic. I'll stay behind. I've got a taser. I'll keep Kim safe if Grace returns for some reason. And once you've saved your daughter, Megan can come back here and finish this very important conversation, which you do not have time for right now. So go. I'm good." Heather raised her nose into the air and glared at us.

I pulled her into a hug. "Have I told you how lucky I am to have you as a best friend today?"

"I know." She returned the hug. "Now, get out of here before I change my mind."

I hugged her again then strode out of the kitchen. Megan, Sarah, and Betty followed me. I paused at the doorway and watched as Heather took a seat at the dinette table. She placed her hand on Kimberly's shoulder as she cried. Kimberly's rough exterior was washed away, and all I saw was a fragile woman who was tired of being let down. I blinked as Charlie jumped up onto the dinette next to them. He curled up next to Kimberly. He was filled with a strange emotion that took me a second to place. *Family.* I didn't know her well enough to think of her like that, but he did. *Why?* He slowly blinked at me and turned away. My familiar was up to something. I cursed under my breath and left. I would have to talk to him about that later. His emotions continued to flow into me through our bond, and before I knew it, I was silently promising Kimberly I would make sure Megan got back soon. Their friendship wasn't beyond repair, and I would make sure they fixed it. Somehow.

CHAPTER 19

I sat perched in the front seat, my eyes glued to my phone, as Betty drove. I directed her through the winding streets of the more affluent neighborhood until we came to a stop in front of Harold's estate. I had seen it only in photos online, where it had looked more impressive. All those photos included a line of cars in the driveway or the building decked out for a glittering party. The home was neat and large, but it seemed lonely somehow. Clearly, it was a sprawling estate for one. Kimberly's car was the only one visible in the driveway. Grace had driven it all the way up to the front door. It sat askew, the front tires halfway into a garden bed.

We parked behind the vehicle. Electricity was in the air, with a strange metallic tang on my tongue. I ran my hands along my arms, trying to brush the hairs back down. But too much magic was in the air for me to calm my nerves. I got out and stalked toward the house. Betty flanked me on the right, Megan on the left, and Sarah followed behind me by a foot. My heart skipped a beat as a green light flashed in the window on the second floor. I ran forward.

"Confess!" Grace yelled, a cold, unrecognizable quality to her voice. She had never sounded so hateful.

I sprinted up the stairs and flung open the door leading into Harold's bedroom. Grace stood in the center of the room, her dark hair swirling around her head as if she were caught in a windstorm. Green sparkles flowed all around her, lighting up the space. Suspended in the air was Harold. He was tall and slender. His once-brown hair was completely gray and had receded, leaving the top of his head bald. He wore silken pajamas, and his gray eyes, brimming with fury, stared at Grace.

"Confess!" Grace yelled again. Green sparkles erupted from her, sending him spinning in the air.

I stepped into the room, my hands out to my sides. "Put him down."

Grace spun toward me. I rolled to the side as she hurled a torrent of magical energy at me. It struck the wooden floor. Chips flew into the air, and one nicked me on my cheek.

"Traitors." Grace stalked toward me.

I scrambled away and reached for Betty. She slipped her hand into mine and linked with Megan. Their power flowed into me as I slammed my other hand down on the ground. Golden light surged forward like a wave. It swept around Grace, forming a globe of light to contain her.

"Traitors!" Grace screamed at the top of her lungs. The house seemed to shift and groan underneath us.

I gasped and forced more of my will into the spell. I had to hold her still, to stop her. We still had time. We still had to have time.

The building groaned again, and the floorboards under my hands convulsed. I stumbled backward as the floorboards heaved under me. I lost concentration for a second, and the globe around Grace vanished. She snarled at me and raised a hand. Green light gathered around her fingertips. Then the room went dark.

Out of instinct, I threw myself to the side. I scrambled along the wall, staring blindly into the darkness. I tried to track her with my ears. Someone groaned, and my head swiveled toward them. *Who was that?* My eyes stung as the room sprang back into view. I squinted at the sudden brightness of it all. Green lights swirled around the room, fighting back against inky-black tendrils. I stared in horror as Delaney and Miranda entered the room with Agnes at their heels.

They're going to take my daughter away. I pushed myself back to my feet. *Is she already gone?* Grace just stood there, wordlessly screaming, as she threw more and more green light at Delaney. She was gaining ground. With each black tendril Delaney threw out, Grace hurled back three streams of green. Miranda pulled out a spell book and read from it, her voice lost to the wind roaring through the room.

Agnes held her hand out toward me, beckoning me over. I ran to her and skidded to a stop by her side. Sarah, Betty, and Megan clustered around. We gripped on to each other. I couldn't take my eyes off Grace. I still couldn't wrap my mind around what I was seeing. I'd known she was possessed, but it was worse than I could have ever imagined.

"They're trying to perform a banishment!" Agnes yelled over the wind and pointed at Miranda. "We need to help her."

"How can we trust them?" I asked.

"We can't," Sarah responded.

"But do we really have a choice?" Betty asked.

Grace's head jerked to the side, and she sneered as she sent a green bolt toward Harold, who was crawling across the ground. Delaney threw up a block at the last second.

We didn't have a choice. Gripping on to Agnes, I stumbled over to Miranda. I put my hand on Miranda's shoulder and gave her my energy to help fuel her spell. Agnes followed suit, followed by Megan. Our power flowed through my body into Miranda. A beam of light, almost pure white, flew from Miranda's chest and struck Grace. It sent her tumbling to the ground. Grace fought against it. I pushed more of my power into Miranda, willing every last bit into the spell. It was my only chance at getting my daughter back. Grace convulsed. A flash of green light spilled out of her mouth and eyes. Grace looked straight at me. "Mom?" She collapsed to the floor.

The room was still. The wind was gone, the green lights vanishing in an instant. The only sound was Harold babbling about how we all needed to leave.

My knees gave out, and I crumpled to the ground.

Miranda closed her book and stowed it inside a hidden pocket in her robes. She strode toward Grace. I pushed myself to my feet and ran forward, throwing myself between them. "You can't take her."

Delaney's laugh filled the room. Miranda cocked her head to the side.

"You can't take her," I said again, stronger this time.

"The threat appears to have been neutralized." Delaney wiped her eyes as she struggled to contain her laughter.

Miranda glanced at Delaney. "We are not in the business of abducting people unnecessarily."

"So you're not here to take her?" I asked.

Delaney straightened. "We need to interview her when she wakes up to see if the Outsider had any accomplices or if it set any other events into motion."

Miranda nodded. "You are free to take her home in the meantime. As my associate said, the threat has been neutralized."

My jaw dropped. *Was it really that simple this whole time?* Delaney's threatening entrance had rattled me. But as I stared into Miranda's eyes, she looked honestly offended at the idea that she might be there to abduct my daughter.

"So we can just go?" I asked.

Miranda beckoned me forward with her finger. With the motion, a white strand of light snaked toward me, wrapping its way around my midsection. I leaned back, but my legs moved toward her against my will. I came to a stop in front of her, and she grabbed my chin, forcing me to look her in the eyes. They were a startling blue. As I stared into them, I felt as if I were falling into them. My breath shuddered. All I could see was their icy-blue depths.

When Miranda spoke, it was as if her voice came at me from every direction. "You will not leave town. You will not flee from our questioning. You will present your daughter to us for interrogation when she wakes. Do you understand?"

My whole body shook as the white tendril flowed into my body. I fought against it, but I couldn't hold the word back. Her magic tore the answer from me. "Yes."

"Your word on it."

My mouth went dry. "I promise."

She released my chin and turned toward Harold. "Now, leave. Sooner rather than later would be preferred. We have some memories of his to fix before the sheriff arrives. My sources tell me they are on their way. It would be inconvenient to have to explain your presence when they get here."

I looked between Miranda and Grace. I wasn't going to take the chance that she might change her mind. Megan darted forward and helped me lift Grace from the ground. Together, we carried her out to Betty's truck. Sarah grabbed Kimberly's keys from Grace's pocket and got into Kimberly's SUV. Betty drove, following her out of the driveway. We turned at the end of the block as we heard sirens blaring in the distance.

I held my daughter's head in my lap as we drove. She was asleep again, but she was back. I felt it in my core. She was my Grace again.

CHAPTER 20

Almost two full days had passed, and Grace still hadn't woken up. Megan and Agnes had both checked on her and said she just needed time to heal. She would wake up soon, and I just had to be patient. Kimberly had lied about not breaking a bone and was back in the hospital. She had fractured her hip. She seemed young to have broken something, but Megan murmured something about the curse and left to go take care of her friend. She'd promised to stay with her until she was well enough to get around again.

After two days of hovering, I'd run out of food at the house. The Retirees were camped out in my guest rooms and had ushered me out with instructions to get enough pie to feed an army. I asked Heather and Chris to meet me at the Slice of Life Diner so that I could have a distraction while I ate real food. They were both waiting for me there with a plate of fries, a grilled cheese sandwich, and Abby's famous tomato soup on the side. I put in an order for pie with Willow then headed over to the booth. I slid in next to Chris and chowed down. Protein bars were great, but they weren't meant to sustain a person.

"How's Grace?" Chris asked.

I grimaced.

He rubbed a hand on my back. "She's going to be okay. She's strong. Just like her mother."

"I can't stay long." I grabbed the grilled cheese and took a massive bite. "Betty's watching her, but I don't want to be gone long. Just in case she wakes up."

Chris nodded. "How about a distraction?"

I smiled. "I could use one."

"We've arrested Harold Mitchell and Benjamin Hayes," Chris said proudly.

"That's great news." Heather clapped.

"What have they been charged with?" I asked.

"We are still going through the evidence we found at Kevin Reynold's place. More charges are being added by the hour. Last I heard, we were up to seventeen counts of first-degree murder."

"Seventeen?" I choked on a fry.

Chris patted me on my back. "Yeah. Unfortunately, the statute of limitations has run out on a lot of stuff, but there isn't one for murder. So we'll at least get him on those. Benjamin flipped. Our case against him is as an accessory to murder, but he's working on a plea deal."

"How's Bob taking it?" I asked.

Chris swallowed. "He's taking a leave of absence. He's put me in charge until he comes back."

Silence settled over the table with a silent *if* to that statement. I didn't like the guy, but I couldn't help but feel bad for him. He had devoted his entire life to being a sheriff. Finding out his dad was crooked must have been a giant blow to his identity.

"But seventeen?" Heather asked, breaking the tension. "Who were the other victims?"

"So far, they've all been people who crossed Harold in a

business deal. And by crossed, I mean didn't do exactly what he wanted."

Heather sat back and pursed her lips. "Why Beau, then? They wouldn't have been in business with each other."

"Harold was the jealous ex-boyfriend," I guessed.

Chris nodded. "He saw Meredith as his property. When she left him, in his book, Beau had stolen her from him."

"Dark." Heather crossed her arms. "Remind me to never date a mobster."

I paused with a fry halfway to my mouth as my conversation with Kevin replayed in my head. "What reason did he give Jim for the murder?"

"He claimed Beau hit Meredith. Jim always liked her, so he thought he was there to protect her honor."

I dropped my fry, finding it hard to continue eating. Harold had made the short list of people I'd met with zero redeeming qualities. It was one person long, and that was saying something after the different murderers I'd faced since moving to Point Pleasant.

"I really should get back. In case Grace wakes up." I glanced at the counter. A box of pies sat on the edge, waiting for me. I couldn't bring myself to continue eating, so I began to box up the leftovers. "Enjoy the rest of your meal. We can do a proper celebratory dinner once she wakes up."

"I'll hold you to it." Chris pulled me into a quick hug.

Heather stood and gave me a hug too. "Call me the second she wakes up."

"I will." I grabbed my to-go bag and walked to the counter. I was standing there, waiting to pay, when the door opened, letting in a cold burst of air.

"Dani?" Imani asked from behind me.

I turned toward her and saw she was dressed in all black, with gold studs in her ears. "Hey. I didn't think I would see you again. You headed back to Georgia?"

She nodded. "Thanks to you, I get to bring Beau's ashes home with answers."

"I'm glad you finally got them," I said.

Her eyes glistened. "Only a year too late. But I'll be interring him in a family plot next to my mom. I like to think she's looking down on us. And with him there with her, she'll finally get the peace she deserves. The peace they both deserve."

Willow called my name. I squeezed Imani's shoulder then stepped up to pay. By the time I was done, she was seated at the bar. I grabbed the pies from the counter and left.

After so many days at Chris's, going back to my own home felt weird. With Grace still unconscious, it didn't entirely feel like home yet. I parked in the driveway and went inside. The Retirees were at the dining room table, playing cards. I dropped the pies off for them and wandered up to my daughter's room. Charlie was lying next to her on her pillow, his body wrapped around her head. He opened a single eye as I entered. I'd moved a recliner into her room that first night. I claimed my normal spot in it and watched her sleep.

"Come back to me, sweetie." I whispered. As an experiment, I sent a mote of magical light into her. I had tried that a few times already with no response. But trying again didn't hurt.

She groaned.

I sat bolt upright in my seat and reached for her. "Grace?" I whispered, sending another mote of light into her.

She rolled toward me and opened her eyes. "Mom?"

"Oh my gosh." I threw myself onto my knees and scrambled to her side.

Grace reached for my hand, tears forming at the corners of her eyes. "Mom. I'm so sorry. I could see what she was doing, but I couldn't stop it."

"It's okay." I kissed her on the forehead. "It's over now."

"No, it's not." She tightened her grip on my hand. "A second before the banishing spell landed, I felt... I felt something break. I don't know what it was. But whatever was inside of me felt happy, and it fled. It's still out there."

Can't wait for the next book? You can get book 8, 'Rituals and the Restless Remains,' here.

In Book 8, Dani Williams is hoping for a quiet stretch in Point Pleasant—but that hope vanishes when the owner of a local occult shop is found murdered. From the moment Dani steps onto the scene, she knows something is wrong. A foul, unfamiliar magic clings to the air, powerful enough to send her instincts—and her stomach—into revolt.

Whatever spell was used, it isn't anything Dani recognizes. Worse, it doesn't behave the way magic should. As she digs deeper, more deaths follow, each one marked by the same unsettling signature. This isn't reckless spellwork or a personal vendetta—it's something deliberate, controlled, and deeply dangerous.

With local law enforcement overwhelmed and no clear magical precedent to follow, Dani is forced to rely on hard-earned experience, careful investigation, and the support of those she trusts most. This time, guessing wrong isn't an option.

As the pattern behind the murders begins to emerge, Dani realizes she's chasing a threat unlike any she's faced before—and uncovering the truth may come at a higher cost than she's prepared to pay.

ALSO BY ELOISE EVERHART

A Williams Witch Mystery

Potions and the Pleasantly Poisoned

Tomes and the Tangled Trail

Divinations and the Disappearing Dead

Hexes and the Haunted House

Spells and the Suspiciously Silent

Grimoires and the Ghostly Guest

Enchantments and the Eerily Ensnared

Rituals and the Restless Remains

Charms and the Cursed Coven

A Miller's Magical Mystery

Murder Among the Hives

Murder Between the Stacks

JOIN MY NEWSLETTER

Interested in receiving bonus content like inspiration character art? If so, join our mailing list and receive access to fun things like 'Foresight and the Fateful Ferry,' and character cards. Go on an adventure with Dani and Chris as they journey into Seattle for a fun day out, and things take a dramatic turn when they stumble upon a dead body on the ferry.

ABOUT THE AUTHOR

Eloise Everhart lives in the Pacific Northwest. Her childhood was marked by voracious reading and tabletop roleplaying games, fueling her lifelong passion for storytelling.

By day, she's a dedicated insurance adjuster. It's a career that has honed her sharp eye for detail and developed her inquisitive mind—a skillset she now seamlessly integrates into her cozy mystery writing.

Beyond her storytelling ardor, Eloise is a devoted wife, sharing her home with a menagerie of rescued cats and dogs who have found their furever home in the Everhart household.

ACKNOWLEDGMENTS

It is hard to believe I am approaching the end of my first series. With only two more books left of the Williams Witch Mystery series I find myself sitting back and contemplating all the help I have received to get here.

My husband has been my rock through the entire process. He has cooked dinners, and taken on more than his fair share of household chores so I can find the time to write. Without him, my journey would have been hopeless.

I also wouldn't have been able to make this book shine without the help of my editors, Rashida Breen and Kelly Reed. This one, more than any others, required a careful threading of the needle to maintain the cozy vibes while still carefully talking about some darker themes. Without your valuable insights, Rashida, the emotional moments wouldn't hit quite as hard. And Kelly, your keen eye really made the prose shine.

To my sister, Andrea. I always appreciate your final pass through before I hit publish. You always seem to catch small things that have made it past so many eyes already. You have my gratitude.

And to my best friend, Andrew, who is no longer with us. I will carry you with me, always.

"Come on a journey with me."

www.ingramcontent.com/pod-product-compliance
Lightning Source LLC
La Vergne TN
LVHW051001080826
845145LV00009B/2395

* 9 7 8 1 9 6 2 7 5 9 0 6 9 *